KT-134-899

VISIONS
OF
SPORT

Celebrating Twenty years of Allsport
The International Sports Picture Agency
IN ASSOCIATION WITH CROSFIELD ELECTRONICS

PELHAM
BOOKS

DEDICATED TO THE EFFORTS OF SPORT AID '88 TO HELP CHILDREN THROUGHOUT THE WORLD

ALLSPORT HAS DONATED ALL ROYALTIES FROM VISIONS OF SPORT TO SUPPORT THE
WORK OF SPORT AID '88, THE GLOBAL CHILDREN'S CHARITY.

THE SINGLE EVENT WHICH CREATED ALLSPORT HAPPENED IN LESS THAN A SECOND. ITS EFFECTS HAVE LASTED TWENTY YEARS.

IN 1968, AT THE MEXICO OLYMPIC GAMES, AMERICAN BOB BEAMON TOOK A FLYING LEAP INTO THE LONG-JUMP SAND-PIT AND LANDED IN HISTORY. HIS JUMP OF 29FT. 2½IN. SMASHED THE WORLD RECORD AND SET A NEW ONE THAT STANDS TO THIS DAY. CROUCHING AT THE END OF THE PIT WAS AN ENGLISH ACCOUNTANT AND PART-TIME PHOTOGRAPHER WHO HAD PAID HIS OWN WAY TO MEXICO.

HIS NAME IS TONY DUFFY AND HIS LIFE, IN THE INSTANT OF BEAMON'S JUMP, WAS CHANGED UTTERLY. DUFFY GOT THE PICTURE. ALLSPORT WAS BORN. IN 1988, VISIONS OF SPORT CELEBRATES ALLSPORT'S TWENTIETH ANNIVERSARY.

THE AGENCY NOW HAS A LIBRARY OF MORE THAN FOUR MILLION COLOUR AND BLACK AND WHITE PICTURES. THEREFORE, TO TRY TO REPRESENT EVEN A FRACTION OF ITS PHOTOGRAPHIC STOCK WOULD BE A FRUITLESS TASK. VISIONS OF SPORT IS NOT, FURTHERMORE, INTENDED AS A PICTORIAL HISTORY OF THE LAST TWENTY YEARS OF WORLD SPORT. NOR IS IT INTENDED TO ILLUSTRATE THE AGENCY'S VAST COLLECTION OF ARCHIVE MATERIAL BECAUSE, TO DO SO, ONE WOULD HAVE TO LOOK FURTHER THAN PHOTOGRAPHS TAKEN SINCE 1968, TO PHOTOGRAPHS DATING AS FAR BACK AS 1885.

WHAT WE HAVE ATTEMPTED TO PRODUCE INSTEAD IS A RECORD OF WHERE ALLSPORT IS NOW. TO THIS END, WE HAVE BASED OUR SELECTION NOT ONLY ON QUALITY OF PHOTOGRAPHY BUT ALSO ON THE VISUAL EXPRESSION OF THE BEAUTY, DRAMA, CONFLICT OR SHEER EMOTION WHICH A SPORTS PHOTOGRAPH MAY PORTRAY.

IN ORDER TO PLACE THE WORK OF THE ALLSPORT PHOTOGRAPHERS IN HISTORICAL CONTEXT, WE HAVE COMMISSIONED TEN ESSAYS, WRITTEN BY LEADING INTERNATIONAL SPORTSWRITERS, ABOUT SOME OF THE PEOPLE WHO HAVE MADE MEMORABLE THE TWO DECADES OF ALLSPORT'S EXISTENCE. WE ARE ALSO GRATEFUL TO IAN WOOLDRIDGE, CHRIS SMITH, JOHN TENNANT AND DALEY THOMPSON, THEMSELVES LEADERS IN THEIR FIELD, FOR WRITING THE INTRODUCTIONS WHICH APPEAR ON THE FOLLOWING PAGES.

DURING 1988 ALLSPORT IS DEMONSTRATING THE DISTANCE TRAVELLED IN THE LAST TWENTY YEARS. AT THE OLYMPICS IN CALGARY AND SEOUL, ALLSPORT'S TEAM OF PHOTOGRAPHERS WILL TAKE MORE THAN 4,000 ROLLS OF FILM AND SERVICE 42 COUNTRIES. SPORTS ILLUSTRATED, LIFE, STERN, SPORTS INTERNATIONAL, L'EQUIPE AND THE OBSERVER MAGAZINE ARE AMONG THOSE WHO WILL PUBLISH ALLSPORT'S WORK.

THUS THIS TWENTY-YEAR CYCLE IS COMPLETED: AT THE 1968 OLYMPIC GAMES IN MEXICO, ALLSPORT WAS FOUNDED ON THE STRENGTH OF ONE PHOTOGRAPH; AT THE 1988 OLYMPIC GAMES IN SEOUL, ALLSPORT PHOTOGRAPHERS WILL TAKE MORE THAN 100,000 PICTURES.

VISIONS OF SPORT IS THE FIRST PART OF THE REST OF THE STORY.

STEVE POWELL, ALLSPORT

I N THE GENIAL ARGOT OF SPORTS JOURNALISM
PHOTOGRAPHERS ARE KNOWN AS SMUDGERS AND REPORTERS ARE CALLED BLUNTS.

For obvious reasons blunts are frequently reluctant to go overboard in praise of smudgers.

It is a question of space: a dynamic picture used boldly across a newspaper page inevitably restricts the wordage available

to the writer working in tandem. he is also conscious of an unchallengeable axiom: one stunning photograph

can generate more impact than 1,000 chiselled words. Just try <u>describing</u> 10 horses mid-air over Becher's Brook.

For years that tended to be more true of war and news reporting than sport.

Specialist sports photographers were rare. More often than not the old office lag was packed off to squat on the dead-ball line

with an even chance of snapping the winning goal.

That changed dramatically a couple of decades ago. A new breed of sports photographer emerged. High marks for technical merit

were taken for granted. The battle was for the highest marks for artistic impression. The winning goal became yesterday's cliche.

How, now, to convey speed, pain, anguish, elation, even death, with startling originality?

It was a whole new lens game demanding imagination, foresight, much planning and a deep knowledge of sport. A handful of

high-performance photographers soared out from the pack, among them the founders of Allsport.

The huge business gamble they took 20 years ago was justified for a simple down-to-earth reason: they never saw artistry as a

substitute for a backbreaking workload. Allsport men ran. They humped more gear than a commando. They worked round the clock.

In two decades their agency has become one of the most prolific and pre-eminent in the world.

As a blunt, I am delighted to celebrate their success in a volume containing so much of their hallmark work.

If they did not invent the new wave they have contributed vitally to it as so many of these pictures will confirm.

Unlike blunts, super-smudgers rarely get a second chance. It is a split-second business and split-second pictorial triumphs

come not by luck but by strategy. Their vast library is a treasure house of examples.

Sport as well as pictorial journalism has reaped a rich reward from Allsport's pursuit of excellence. I recall as a child being drawn

to sport, and later sportswriting, by a single photograph. It was a black-and-white

panoramic view of a packed Sydney Cricket Ground transfixed by one of the Bodyline Test matches and was the wrap-around

dust jacket on Sir Pelham Warner's Book of Cricket. It conveyed heat, tension and high drama and inspired a schoolboy to

become part of that thrilling world, albeit in a lowly bluntish role.

That picture was taken 56 years ago and literally transformed one human life. By the same process I suspect Allsport

may have changed more lives than they will ever know.

IAN WOOLDRIDGE

P HOTOGRAPHY IS ABOUT "SEEING" —
VISUALISING THE SUBJECT AS THE FINISHED
PICTURE. IT IS ISOLATING IN THE MIND'S EYE
THE FRACTION OF A SECOND FROM AN EVENT THAT
INTERPRETS THE SUBJECT IN A WAY WHICH IS
PHOTOGRAPHICALLY INTERESTING AND WHICH
EXPRESSES THE EVENT'S OR SUBJECT'S OWN PERSONALITY.

"SEEING" REQUIRES THE PHOTOGRAPHER TO USE THE EYE AS A LENS. THE LENS RECORDS EVERYTHING WITHIN ITS FIELD OF VIEW WHILE THE EYE IS MORE SELECTIVE, FOCUSING ONLY ON THINGS THAT INTEREST IT. IN THIS RESPECT THE PHOTOGRAPHER SEEKS TO TEACH THE EYE TO SEE LIKE A CAMERA LENS AND TO PAY ATTENTION TO EVERYTHING IN ITS FIELD OF VIEW.

A PHOTOGRAPH BRINGS TOGETHER MANY THINGS, PEOPLE, OBJECTS AND SCENES AND REPRESENTS THEM AT A GIVEN MOMENT IN TIME. IN SPORT THE PROBLEMS OF A PHOTOGRAPHER ARE HEIGHTENED AS THE SUBJECT IS OFTEN MOVING AT HIGH SPEED.

THE SPORTS PICTURE SEEKS TO TAKE A PART OF AN EVENT (MAYBE 1,000TH OF A SECOND), MAKE IT REPRESENTATIVE OF THE WHOLE AND MAKE IT AESTHETICALLY APPEALING WHILST RETAINING A FEELING OF MOVEMENT AND OF THE EVENT ITSELF. TO DO THIS THE PHOTOGRAPHER MUST HAVE AN UNDERSTANDING OF THE RULES OF THE EVENT BEING COVERED AND, OF COURSE, A THOROUGH KNOWLEDGE OF HIS CAMERAS AND EQUIPMENT.

THE CHOICES FACING THE PHOTOGRAPHER ARE VAST. DO YOU CHOOSE THE WHOLE OF THE SUBJECT OR A DETAIL IN CLOSE-UP? A HIGH OR A LOW VIEWPOINT? DO YOU USE A WIDE ANGLE OR A TELEPHOTO? DO YOU FREEZE THE ACTION OR BLUR FOR EFFECT? DO YOU CHOOSE VIBRANT COLOURS OR PASTELS? IT IS THE SELECTION FROM THESE OPTIONS THAT ALLOWS THE PHOTOGRAPHER TO PUT HIS OR HER INTERPRETATION ON THE EVENT — IN SHORT HOW HE OR SHE "SEES" — AND IT IS THIS THAT GIVES SPORTS PICTURES THEIR GREAT DIVERSITY AND INTEREST.

OUTSIDE INFLUENCES SUCH AS POOR LIGHT CAN OFTEN RESTRICT THE PHOTOGRAPHER BUT I BELIEVE WHEREVER POSSIBLE HE OR SHE SHOULD ALWAYS BE ADVENTUROUS AND WORK ON THE EDGE, LOOKING FOR THE NEW VIEWPOINT OR FOR SOMETHING FRESH TO SAY.

ALLSPORT PHOTOGRAPHERS SEEK TO APPLY THESE CRITERIA TO THEIR WORK AT ALL LEVELS. THEIR INTERNATIONAL STANDING AS WELL AS THEIR REPUTATION AT HOME IS RECOGNITION OF THIS.

Chris Smith

CHRIS SMITH

I HAVE WORKED WITH ALLSPORT ON MANY OCCASIONS OVER THE LAST DECADE – INITIALLY AS ART EDITOR AT THE SUNDAY TIMES MAGAZINE AND LATER AS ART DIRECTOR FOR THE OBSERVER MAGAZINE. WHILST ALLSPORT PRESENT PORTFOLIOS OF EXCELLENT FEATURES CONSISTENTLY, IT IS

THEIR APPROACH AND DEDICATION TO THE BIG STORY THAT STANDS OUT. TO DATE, WE HAVE COLLABORATED ON TWO WORLD CUPS (ARGENTINA 1978 AND MEXICO 1986) THE LOS ANGELES OLYMPICS, 1984, THE ROME WORLD ATHLETICS CHAMPIONSHIPS, 1987, AND THE CALGARY WINTER OLYMPICS, 1988. ALL THESE PROJECTS DEMANDED NOT ONLY THE VERY BEST IN SPORT ACTION PHOTOGRAPHY, BUT ALSO A HIGH DEGREE OF ORGANISATION IN ORDER TO GET THOSE PICTURES TO EDITORS WAITING AGAINST DEADLINES ALL AROUND THE WORLD. I WILL NEVER FORGET THE HIVE OF ROUND-THE-CLOCK BACKROOM ACTIVITY IN LOS ANGELES DURING THE '84 OLYMPICS. FOR ME, AS AN ART DIRECTOR, ASSEMBLING REPORTAGES OF MAJOR EVENTS LIKE THESE DEMANDS NOT ONLY PICTURES OF WINNERS BUT ALSO ATMOSPHERE AND GRAND CHANGES OF SCALE WITHIN PHOTOGRAPHS. IT GOES WITHOUT SAYING THAT ALL THESE FACTORS ARE ACCOMPANIED BY THOSE PRE-REQUISITES; STRONG COMPOSITION, SHARP FOCUS AND CORRECT EXPOSURE.

ALLSPORT MAINTAIN A HIGH STRIKE RATE WHEN IT COMES TO GETTING THESE IMAGES – WHETHER IT IS THE HARD, SHARP, QUINTESSENTIAL MOMENT DURING COMPETITION, THE MORE REFLECTIVE PHOTOGRAPH THAT CAPTURES A TELLING MOOD OR THE MORE "GRAPHIC" SHOT THAT LOOKS SO STYLISH ON THE PAGE.

BOTH BEHIND THE CAMERA AND BEHIND THE SCENES, ALLSPORT DELIVER THE GOODS.

John Tennant

JOHN TENNANT

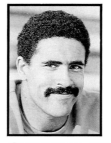

A

CHIEVING BETTER THAN AVERAGE PHOTOGRAPHS ON A CONSISTENT BASIS IS A LITTLE MORE INVOLVED THAN MOST PEOPLE REALISE.

99 TIMES OUT OF 100 YOU GET ONLY ONE CHANCE.

SO, BEFORE YOU EVEN GET YOUR FINGER NEAR THE SHUTTER AT A MAJOR SPORTS EVENT YOU HAVE TO HAVE GONE THROUGH THE SIX PS:

PREVIEW – DO YOUR HOMEWORK.

PREPARE – PLAN YOUR SHOTS AND PREPARE YOUR EQUIPMENT.

POSITION – LEARN TO BE IN THE RIGHT PLACE AT THE RIGHT TIME.

PERSISTENCE – LEARN FROM SUCCESSES AND FAILURES.

PRACTICE – DO IT, DO IT, DO IT AND HAVE PHUN!!

THESE PS APPLY TO EVERYTHING IN LIFE IF YOU WANT TO GET AHEAD. WHEN IT COMES TO SPORTS PHOTOGRAPHY, ALLSPORT STAND OUT FROM THE CROWD BECAUSE I HAVE SEEN THEM APPLY THESE PRINCIPLES CONSISTENTLY AND WELL, THUS PRODUCING PROBABLY THE BEST PHOTOGRAPHERS IN THE WORLD.

SPORTS PHOTOGRAPHY IS COMPETITIVE. THE PHOTOGRAPHER OFTEN HAS TO ARRIVE AT A VENUE MANY HOURS BEFORE THE COMPETITOR IN ORDER TO GET THE BEST SITE. THIS MAY BE AT 5.30 IN THE MORNING IN PITCH BLACK WITH MINUS 30 DEGREES C TEMPERATURES WHERE FILMS CRACK AND FINGERS STICK TO CAMERAS. EVEN WORSE, AS ALLSPORT PHOTOGRAPHERS HAVE FOUND OUT, IT MAY MEAN HAVING TO SPEND FOUR TO FIVE DAYS WITH SOMEONE LIKE ME!

FOR THE PHOTOGRAPHER, TAKING SPORTS PICTURES IS AN ATTEMPT TO COMMUNICATE THE EXCITEMENT THAT HE SEES AND FEELS. THAT IS WHAT MAKES TAKING SPORTS PHOTOGRAPHS SPECIAL AND ALSO FAR MORE DIFFICULT THAN THE BEST PHOTOGRAPHERS MAKE IT LOOK. FOR THE ATHLETE, SPORTS PHOTOGRAPHS PROVIDE A LASTING MOMENTO OF A PAST EVENT BUT IT IS ALSO TRUE THAT THE PHOTOGRAPHER'S VISION CAN PROVIDE INSPIRATION AND MOTIVATION.

DALEY THOMPSON

ANDREW JAMESON, ORLANDO, FLORIDA, 1985.

PHOTOGRAPH BY BOB MARTIN

INTENSITY OF ATMOSPHERE IN THE OLYMPIC GYMNASTIC ARENA CAN MOISTEN THE PALMS OF THE COOLEST COMPETITOR. CHALKING THE PALM IS NOT ONLY A NECESSARY PIECE OF THE RITUAL BUT ALSO ALLOWS A MOMENT IN WHICH TO FOCUS MIND AND BODY. ONE SLIP CAN MEAN DISASTER.

MAIN PHOTOGRAPH BY BOB MARTIN

GRIP IS JUST AS ESSENTIAL FOR TIMOTHY DAGGETT (ABOVE) VAULTING FOR THE USA AT THE LOS ANGELES OLYMPICS, 1984

PHOTOGRAPH BY STEVE POWELL

FOR THE USA TEAM (BELOW), WHO TOOK THE OVERALL GOLD MEDAL IN LOS ANGELES, ELATION SPEAKS LOUDER THAN WORDS. PHOTOGRAPH BY STEVE POWELL

DIEGO ARMANDO MARADONA, MEXICO 1986. THE VICTORIOUS ARGENTINA CAPTAIN FOUND THE WORLD AT HIS FEET. THERE WERE OCCASIONS (MAIN PICTURE) WHEN THE SITUATIONS CREATED BY SUCH AN AWESOME TALENT REQUIRED DESPERATE MEASURES. IN THE WORLD CUP FINAL, HOWEVER, WEST GERMANY CAPITULATED AS HAD ENGLAND BEFORE THEM. PHOTOGRAPH BY GERARD VANDYSTADT. IN SPAIN, FOUR YEARS EARLIER, BELGIUM FOUND A WAY OF SUFFOCATING MARADONA'S OBVIOUS POTENTIAL (ABOVE RIGHT) ON THEIR WAY TO A 1-0 VICTORY OVER ARGENTINA. PHOTOGRAPH BY BY STEVE POWELL. BY 1986 HE HAD ADDED EXPERIENCE TO TALENT. ONE QUALITY REMAINED GLORIOUSLY FRESH IN HIS HURDLING OF TACKLES (ABOVE LEFT) AND HIS HUGGING OF TEAM-MATES (TOP LEFT) – EXUBERANCE. PHOTOGRAPHS BY DAVID CANNON.

RACHEL MCLISH (RIGHT) TWICE MISS OLYMPIA. PHOTOGRAPH BY TONY DUFFY. **THE POWER AND POISE OF WOMEN'S BODY-BUILDING (BELOW).** PHOTOGRAPH BY MIKE POWELL

MICHAEL O'CONNOR OF THE UNSTOPPABLE AUSTRALIANS. WHO ILLUMINATED RUBGY LEAGUE IN 1986.

PREPARES TO KICK FOR GOAL IN THE 34-4 VICTORY OVER ENGLAND. PHOTOGRAPH BY SIMON BRUTY.

18

THE APPARENTLY MORE GENTLE PURSUIT OF BOULES OCCUPIES THE
ATTENTION DURING THE JEU PROVENCAL, 1987. PHOTOGRAPH BY CHRISTIAN PETIT.

FROZEN IN MOTION. STUDY IN WHITE AS WEST
GERMANY'S SNOW QUEEN MARINA KIEHL RIDES ON THE
EDGE DURING THE CALGARY WINTER OLYMPICS, 1988.
PHOTOGRAPH BY STEVE POWELL.

BASEBALL – ABOUT AS AMERICAN AS YOU CAN GET. BUT UNIVERSITY OF SOUTHERN CALIFORNIA
VERSUS TAIWAN? HAT'S OFF TO THAT (RIGHT). NOT QUITE A CATCHER'S EYE VIEW OF THE LOS ANGELES
DODGERS IN PRACTICE DURING THE 1985 SEASON (ABOVE). PHOTOGRAPH BY MIKE POWELL.

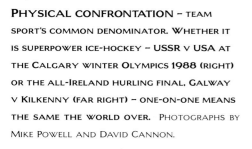

PHYSICAL CONFRONTATION – TEAM SPORT'S COMMON DENOMINATOR. WHETHER IT IS SUPERPOWER ICE-HOCKEY – USSR V USA AT THE CALGARY WINTER OLYMPICS 1988 (RIGHT) OR THE ALL-IRELAND HURLING FINAL, GALWAY V KILKENNY (FAR RIGHT) – ONE-ON-ONE MEANS THE SAME THE WORLD OVER. PHOTOGRAPHS BY MIKE POWELL AND DAVID CANNON.

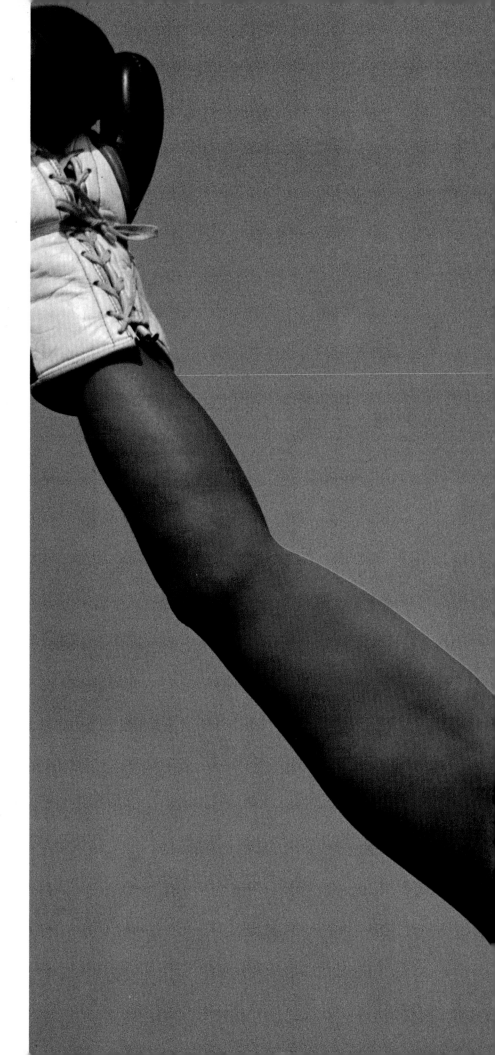

MAYBE THE ONLY HEAVYWEIGHT IN HISTORY WHO COULD HAVE BEATEN CASSIUS CLAY WAS MUHAMMAD ALI. CONSIDERING THEY WERE ONE AND THE SAME PERSON THAT STATEMENT MAY SOUND AN ABSURDITY, BUT IN BOXING TERMS IT IS A LEGITIMATE ASSERTION.

CASSIUS CLAY, THE HANDS-DANGLING, QUICKSILVER INNOVATOR WHO DANCED HIS WAY FIRST TO THE OLYMPIC LIGHT-HEAVYWEIGHT GOLD MEDAL AT THE ROME OLYMPICS IN 1960 AND THEN TO THE WORLD HEAVYWEIGHT TITLE AT 21, WAS VIRTUALLY IMPOSSIBLE TO HIT. APART FROM A FEW BRIEF SECONDS AGAINST OUR OWN HENRY COOPER IN THE NOTORIOUS 'SPLIT GLOVE' AFFAIR IN 1963, HE NEVER ONCE LOOKED IN DANGER OF BEING BEATEN.

BUT BY THE TIME HE RESUMED HIS CAREER IN 1970, AFTER A PROLONGED BATTLE WITH THE US GOVERNMENT OVER HIS REFUSAL TO ACCEPT INDUCTION INTO THE ARMY HAD COST HIM HIS CHAMPIONSHIP AND THE THREE BEST YEARS OF HIS CAREER, HE HAD BECOME A POLITICALLY-AWARE BLACK ACTIVIST CALLED MUHAMMAD ALI, AND WAS A VASTLY DIFFERENT FIGHTER.

ALI WAS THE MOST ADAPTABLE HEAVYWEIGHT THE SPORT HAS EVER SEEN. IN THE END, IT WAS AGE AND EGO THAT TOPPLED HIM. LIKE SO MANY OTHER RING LEGENDS, HE COULD NOT ACCEPT THE EVIDENCE OF HIS OWN PHYSICAL DETERIORATION. BUT EVEN TOWARDS THE END, THE OLD MASTER WAS STILL CAPABLE OF SUMMONING UP STUNNING PERFORMANCES LIKE THE ONE WITH WHICH HE REGAINED THE TITLE FOR AN UNPRECEDENTED SECOND TIME FROM THE YOUNG UPSTART, LEON SPINKS, IN NEW ORLEANS IN SEPTEMBER 1978. THAT SHOULD HAVE BEEN THE TIME FOR HIM TO LEAVE, BUT INSTEAD HE EMBARRASSED HIMSELF AND AN ARMY OF FANS WITH FUMBLING DISPLAYS AGAINST LARRY HOLMES AND TREVOR BERBICK BEFORE, AT 38, FINALLY HAVING TO ACCEPT THAT EVEN HIS UNIQUE GENIUS HAD ITS LIMITS.

NO FIGHTER IN HISTORY HAS EVER STIRRED THE EMOTIONS IN QUITE THE SAME WAY. HIS APPEAL WAS TRULY INTERNATIONAL, PROBABLY BECAUSE HE, UNLIKE SO MANY OF HIS PREDECESSORS, REGARDED THE CHAMPIONSHIP AS BELONGING TO THE WORLD RATHER THAN JUST TO AMERICA. HE TOOK THE TITLE ON THE ROAD, AND DEFENDED IT ANYWHERE A CHALLENGER COULD BE FOUND. HIS OUTSPOKEN STANCE ON RACIAL MATTERS AND ON AMERICAN INVOLVEMENT IN THE VIETNAM WAR ("I AIN'T GOT NO QUARREL WITH THEM VIET CONG … THEY NEVER CALLED ME NIGGER") MADE HIM FIRST VILLAIN AND THEN MARTYR IN HIS HOME COUNTRY. HIS VERY PUBLIC OPPOSITION TO THE WAR, AT INCALCULABLE PERSONAL AND FINANCIAL COST, DID MUCH TO SWING AMERICAN PUBLIC OPINION AGAINST IT.

ALI, OF ALL PEOPLE, SHOULD HAVE BEEN ABLE TO ENJOY IN THE SECOND HALF OF HIS LIFE THE FRUITS OF HIS FIRST FABULOUS 40 YEARS, BUT THE DISEASE WHICH ULTIMATELY WREAKED SUCH APPALLING CHANGES IN HIM WAS ALREADY EATING AWAY AT HIM IN THE FINAL YEARS OF HIS CAREER. TODAY, HE IS STILL PRODUCED AT BIG-FIGHT OCCASIONS, AND ALWAYS THE AFFECTIONATE CHANT OF "ALI, ALI" SWELLS AROUND THE ARENA. BUT THERE IS A SAD ECHO OF ANOTHER GREAT BLACK CHAMPION, JOE LOUIS, WHOSE LIFE PETERED OUT IN A DISTASTEFUL ROUND OF PAID PUBLIC APPEARANCES.

BOXING DOES NOT DESERVE THE HEROES IT GETS, NOR DO THEY DESERVE THE TREAT-MENT THAT TOO MANY OF THEM RECEIVE FROM IT. **HARRY MULLAN** BOXING NEWS

MUHAMMAD ALI, 1972. DUBLIN, DURING TRAINING FOR HIS FIGHT WITH AL "BLUE" LEWIS. PHOTOGRAPH BY DON MORLEY.

FIRE AND ICE AT THE CALGARY WINTER
OLYMPICS, 1988. THE OLYMPIC FLAME
(ABOVE) BURNS ITS MESSAGE: "FASTER,
HIGHER, FURTHER" WHILE COMPETITORS IN
THE TWO-MAN BOBSLEIGH (RIGHT) FIGHT
TO CHISEL OUT HUNDREDTHS OF SECONDS
FROM THE FROZEN, UNYIELDING WALL.
PHOTOGRAPHS BY PASCAL RONDEAU AND
GUIDO BENETTON.

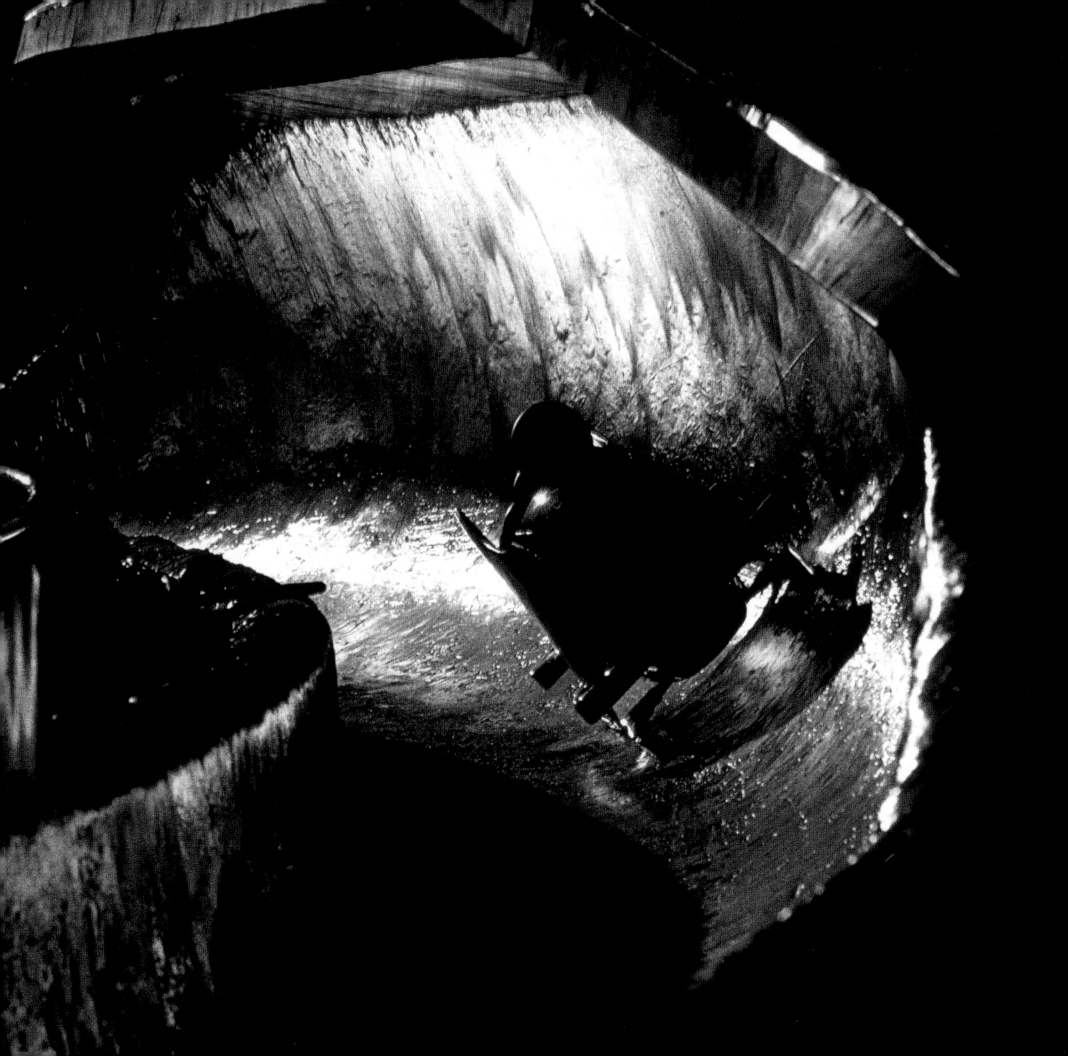

IN THE 1984 BRITISH OPEN AT ST. ANDREWS, VICTORY FOR SEVERIANO BALLESTEROS REQUIRED A
BIRDIE PUTT ON THE FINAL GREEN. SEVE'S REACTION (ABOVE): "VAYA! VAYA! VAYA!" – ROUGHLY
TRANSLATED AS "WOW!" – COMPLETES THE STORY. PHOTOGRAPHS BY DAVE CANNON.
DURING THE 1986 FRENCH OPEN AT LA BOULIE (RIGHT), BALLESTEROS PEERS ANXIOUSLY AROUND AN
OVERHANGING BRANCH TO DISCOVER IF HE HAS ESCAPED FROM THE ROUGH. HE HAD.
PHOTOGRAPH BY JEAN-MARC LOUBAT.

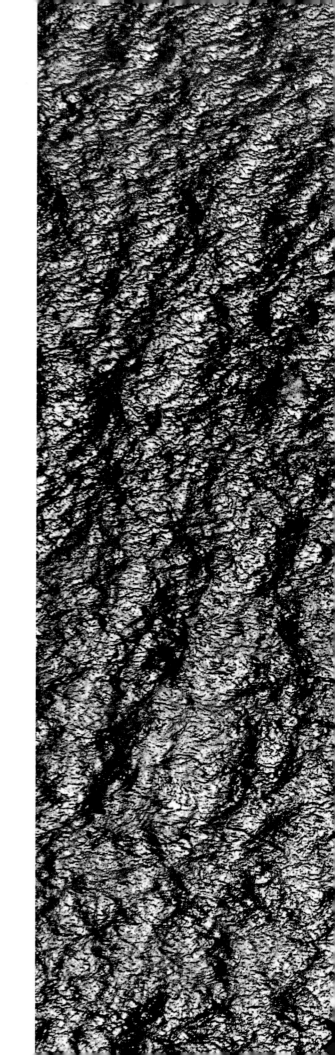

THE MIRROR IMAGE CREATED BY PERFECT UNDERWATER SYNCHRONISATION. AMERICA'S GOLD MEDALLISTS TRACEY RUIZ AND CANDY COSTEE (ABOVE) DEMONSTRATE THE ART OF THE GRACEFUL AND THE WEIGHTLESS IN THE 1984 LOS ANGELES OLYMPICS POOL, WHERE THEIR SPORT BECAME AN OLYMPIC EVENT FOR THE FIRST TIME. PHOTOGRAPH BY STEVE POWELL.
PETER BLAKES' TRIMARAN, STEINLAGER (RIGHT), CUTS THE WAVES IN A TWO-HANDED RACE ACROSS THE SOUTH PACIFIC, OFF THE COAST OF NEW ZEALAND. PHOTOGRAPH BY OLI TENNENT.

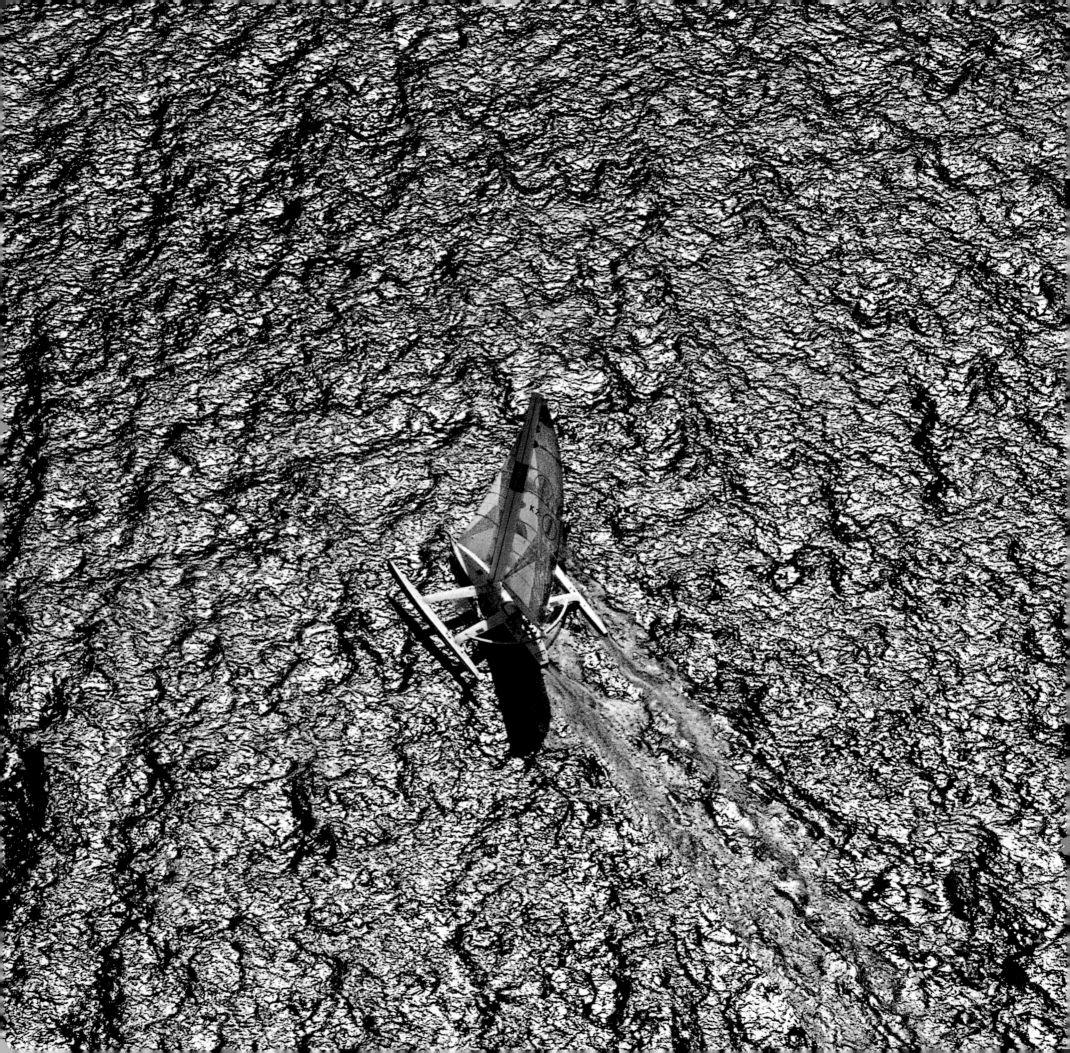

BEN JOHNSON OF CANADA. AT THE 1987 WORLD CHAMPIONSHIPS IN ROME, JOHNSON PROVED HIMSELF SIMPLY THE FASTEST MAN ALIVE. AFTER SETTING A NEW 100 METRES WORLD RECORD (9.83 SECONDS), THE ENORMITY OF HIS ACHIEVEMENT SOAKS INTO HIS MEMORY (ABOVE). PHOTOGRAPH BY TONY DUFFY.

SOON AFTERWARDS JOHNSON REVERTS TO BEING A TAUT SPRING OF TENSION (RIGHT) AS HE BURSTS FROM THE BLOCKS IN THE 4x100 METRES RELAY. EXPLOSIVE POWER HARNESSED PERFECTLY. PHOTOGRAPH BY JEAN-MARC BAREY.

THE PATIENCE AND THE PAIN. BJORN BORG, OF SWEDEN, UNDENIABLY THE GREATEST MEN'S TENNIS PLAYER OF HIS GENERATION – POSSIBLY OF ALL TIME – PREPARES TO SERVE AT WIMBLEDON, 1980 (ABOVE). PHOTOGRAPH BY STEVE POWELL.

IVAN LENDL, CZECHOSLOVAKIA (RIGHT), DESPITE HIS STATUS AS NUMBER ONE FOLLOWING THE RETIREMENT OF BORG AND THE DISENCHANTMENT OF JOHN MCENROE, NEVER MANAGED TO DUPLICATE THE SWEDE'S MASTERY OF GRASS. HIS EYES ARE THE EYES OF A MAN FOR WHOM GREATNESS IS NEAR ENOUGH TO TOUCH BUT TOO FAR AWAY TO POSSESS.

PHOTOGRAPH BY TREVOR JONES.

**IN ENGLAND'S GREEN AND
PLEASANT LAND . . . HENLEY (ABOVE).**
THE CROWD AT THE WORLD'S MOST FAMOUS
ROWING REGATTA TRY NOT TO LET ALL
THAT EXERCISE DISTRACT THEM FROM
MATTERS MORE IMMEDIATE.
PHOTOGRAPH BY ADRIAN MURRELL.
LEEDS CASTLE, KENT (RIGHT), WHERE THE
BALLOON GOES UP IN A STUNNING SETTING.
PHOTOGRAPH BY PASCAL RONDEAU.

A YEAR OR TWO AGO, SEBASTIAN COE TRAVELLED TO COVENTRY TO WATCH CHELSEA PLAY A FIRST DIVISION FOOTBALL MATCH. THE TRAIN FROM LONDON WAS DELAYED AND, SHORTLY BEFORE THE KICK-OFF, HUNDREDS OF CHELSEA FANS ARRIVED AT HIGHFIELD ROAD, CLAMOURING FOR ADMISSION. THE GATE-MAN, WITH THAT SADISTIC GLEE PECULIAR TO HIS TRADE, INFORMED THEM THAT THEIR ENTRANCE WAS ON THE FAR SIDE OF THE GROUND. EVENTUALLY COE, WITH A TICKET TO COLLECT, REACHED THE FRONT OF THE CROWD. "CHELSEA FANS, FAR SIDE," SAID THE GATE-MAN. A DESPERATE COE SAID: "LOOK, THERE'S A TICKET WAITING FOR ME ON THIS GATE. THE NAME'S SEBASTIAN COE." THE GATE-MAN WAS UTTERLY UNIMPRESSED. "FAR SIDE," HE SAID. "AND WITH A NAME LIKE THAT, IT SHOULDN'T TAKE YOU LONG TO GET ROUND THERE."

COE TELLS THIS STORY ONLY WHEN PROMPTED BUT EVEN HE MUST FIND IT DIFFICULT TO BELIEVE THAT ANYBODY WHO HAS LIVED IN BRITAIN FOR THE PAST DECADE COULD NOT INSTANTLY PUT A NAME TO THAT FAMILIAR FACE. IN THE PUBLIC EYE, SEB COE CEASED TO BE A MERE ATHLETE SEVERAL YEARS AGO. IT IS A PERCEPTION THAT DOES HIM LESS THAN JUSTICE. COE HAS NEVER SEEN HIMSELF AS A 'MERE' ATHLETE. HE IS AN ATHLETE FIRST, FOREMOST AND FOR AS LONG AS HIS LEGS CAN GENERATE EXTRAORDINARY PACE.

THERE ARE THOSE WHO INSIST THAT COE COULD NEVER ENLIST UNIVERSAL AFFECTION FOR HIS EFFORTS BECAUSE HE MADE THE VERY ACT OF RUNNING APPEAR FAR TOO SIMPLE. YET COE KNEW WHAT OTHERS HAD VAGUELY GUESSED – THAT THE ABILITY TO FLOAT, ACCELERATE AND KICK OFF THE PACE WAS THE PRODUCT OF AN AGONISINGLY UNREASONABLE WORK LOAD. WHEN THE WORLD RECORDS CAME, AND THEY CAME IN BEWILDERING PROFUSION, HE WAS REAPING THE REWARDS OF A TRAINING SCHEDULE WHICH ONLY MEN LIKE THOMPSON, CRAM OR OVETT COULD COMPREHEND.

SADLY, IT IS THE FATE OF ATHLETES TO BE TREATED LIKE SENIOR CITIZENS BEFORE THEY REACH THE AGE OF 30. I RECALL A TEENAGE MEMBER OF THE BRITISH TEAM BEING INTRODUCED TO COE AT THE EUROPEAN CHAMPIONSHIPS IN STUTTGART. "SEB COE!", SHE SAID. "MY DAD'S TOLD ME ABOUT YOU." HE SMILED THE TIGHT LITTLE SMILE HE EMPLOYS WHEN CHELSEA LOSE AT HOME. BEFORE HIS CAREER WAS OVER, IT WAS BEING USHERED INTO HISTORY. YET HISTORY IS DESTINED TO GAPE AND GOGGLE AT THE PERFORMANCES WHICH SPATTERED THAT GLITTERING CAREER. IT WILL TELL OF THE THREE WORLD RECORDS SET IN THE SPACE OF SIX SUMMER WEEKS IN 1979. IT WILL SPEAK IN HUSHED TONES OF THAT EVENING IN FLORENCE, WHEN HE RAN 800 METRES IN 1 MIN 41.72 SECS TO SET A RECORD WHICH REMAINS DAUNTINGLY INTACT. AND IT WILL RELATE MOST PROUDLY THE TALE OF THE TWO OLYMPIC 1,500 METRES TITLES; THE FIRST IN MOSCOW, WON BY DOGGED STRENGTH OF CHARACTER; THE SECOND, IN LOS ANGELES, DELIVERED THROUGH SUBLIME EFFICIENCY.

PATRICK COLLINS MAIL ON SUNDAY

SEBASTIAN COE, WINNING HIS OLYMPIC 1500 METRES GOLD MEDALS: IN LOS ANGELES 1984 (RIGHT). PHOTOGRAPH BY STEVE POWELL. IN MOSCOW 1980 (FAR RIGHT). PHOTOGRAPH BY TONY DUFFY.

PATHOS. BARRY MCGUIGAN (LEFT) LOSES HIS WORLD FEATHERWEIGHT TITLE TO STEVE CRUZ IN LAS VEGAS, 1986. PHOTOGRAPH BY MIKE POWELL.
POWER. TONY SIBSON (RIGHT) LOSES HIS SENSES IN A COMEBACK CRACK AT FRANK TATE'S IBF MIDDLEWEIGHT TITLE, 1988. PHOTOGRAPH BY RUSSELL CHEYNE.

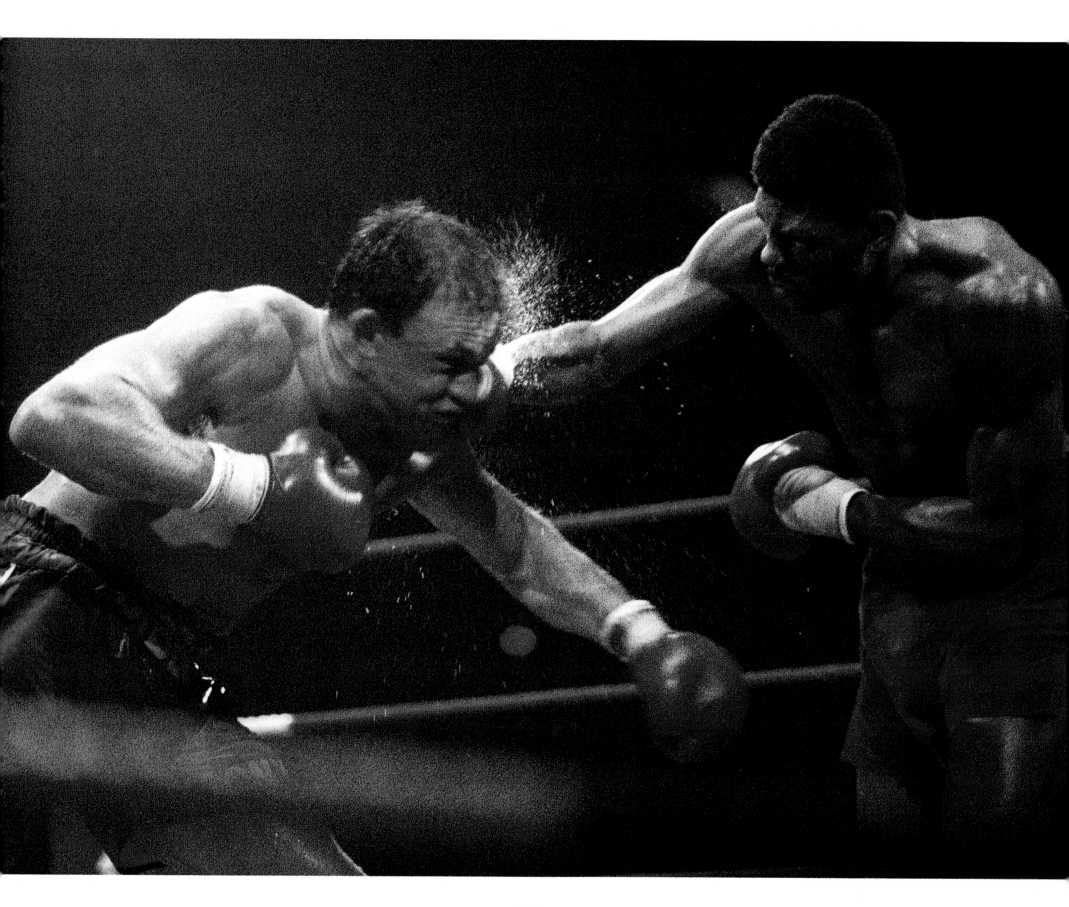

TO THE LIMIT. FRANZ CARR
APPEARS IN DANGER OF DECAPITATION
BY MARK FALCO'S OUTSTRETCHED
BOOT (RIGHT) – WATFORD V
NOTTINGHAM FOREST, 1987.
PHOTOGRAPH BY DAN SMITH.

AT THE MEXICO WORLD CUP IN 1986
GARY LINEKER (FAR RIGHT) AND
ENGLAND KEPT THEIR HEADS AFTER A
DISASTROUS START TO THE
COMPETITION TO BEAT POLAND AND
START A CHARGE WHICH ENDED IN THE
QUARTER-FINAL AGAINST ARGENTINA.
PHOTOGRAPH BY MIKE KING.

GRACE, ATHLETICISM AND DELICACY – Debi Thomas of the United States, the former world champion free-skater, is a vision on ice. Photograph by Bob Martin.

THE ITALIAN TEAM, 4000 METRE TEAM PURSUIT, 1986 WORLD
CHAMPIONSHIPS, COLORADO. PHOTOGRAPH BY MIKE POWELL.

THE VAGARIES OF LIFE IN THE FAST LANE. ALAIN PROST, "THE PROFESSOR," MAKES TIME STAND STILL DURING THE 1987 AUSTRALIAN GRAND PRIX IN ADELAIDE. UNFORTUNATELY FOR THE FRENCH 1985 AND 1986 WORLD CHAMPION, BRAKE PROBLEMS BROUGHT HIS MACHINE TO A STANDSTILL ON THE 54TH LAP. PHOTOGRAPH BY SIMON BRUTY.

SPLASHING OUT. JOANNA WINTER LOSES CONTACT WITH STAINLESS STEEL AT THE 1975 BADMINTON HORSE TRIALS, SHORTLY BEFORE BEING LANDED ON BY HER MOUNT. SHE SUFFERED RELATIVELY MINOR INJURIES WHILE THE HORSE, OF COURSE, WAS COMPLETELY UNSCATHED. PHOTOGRAPH BY TONY DUFFY.

MUD AND THUNDER FOR THE BRITISH LIONS RUGBY TOURISTS AGAINST
NEW ZEALAND JUNIORS IN WELLINGTON, 1977.
PHOTOGRAPH BY ADRIAN MURRELL

A MOMENT TO REFLECT FOR
BRITAIN'S NICK FALDO (RIGHT) AT THE
1984 US MASTERS IN AUGUSTA, GEORGIA.
PHOTOGRAPH BY DAVID CANNON
AND FOR ZHANG OF CHINA (FAR RIGHT)
IN THE WOMEN'S 300 METRE SPEED
SKATING AT THE 1988 CALGARY WINTER
OLYMPICS. PHOTOGRAPH BY MIKE POWELL.

A MAN ALONE WITH HIS DESIRE TO SUCCEED. HENRY MATHERS (USA) PUTS IN THE
LENGTHS AT THE PRACTICE POOL, MISSION BAY, FLORIDA. PHOTOGRAPH BY BOB MARTIN.

MARTINA NAVRATILOVA HAS HAD TO OVERCOME ALL MANNER OF OBSTACLES, INCLUDING PREJUDICE AND A PREDILECTION FOR JUNK FOOD, IN ORDER TO BECOME THE RICHEST WOMAN IN SPORT. EVERY FINELY-TUNED SINEW SUGGESTS THAT THE BLESSING OF TALENT WAS ALLIED TO A STRONG WILL AND PERHAPS EVEN A KEEN SENSE OF INJUSTICE. NO TENNIS PLAYER OF EITHER SEX HAS WON MORE OFFICIAL PRIZE MONEY THAN THE 13 MILLION DOLLARS NAVRATILOVA HAS EARNED SINCE DEFECTING TO THE UNITED STATES FROM CZECHOSLOVAKIA IN 1975. IN THE BRIEF RESPITE BETWEEN TOURNAMENTS, SHE CAN RELAX IN HOMES IN FORT WORTH, TEXAS AND ASPEN, COLORADO. IN COMMON WITH IVAN LENDL, THE LEADING MALE PLAYER, WHO HAS ALSO BASED HIMSELF AND HIS FORTUNE IN AMERICA, SHE LOOKS BACK ON LIFE IN HER HOMELAND WITH MIXED FEELINGS.

HER MOTHER AND FATHER DIVORCED WHEN SHE WAS THREE YEARS OLD, AND SHE WENT TO LIVE IN A SINGLE ROOM AT HER MOTHER'S CHILDHOOD HOME JUST OUTSIDE PRAGUE. THE ROOM OVERLOOKED A NEGLECTED RED CLAY TENNIS COURT, WHICH WAS ALL THAT REMAINED OF HER MOTHER'S FAMILY ESTATE. BEFORE THE COMMUNISTS TOOK CONTROL IN 1948, THEY POSSESSED 30 ACRES OF LAND. NOW THE FAMILY HAD TO SHARE THEIR HOUSE WITH OTHER PEOPLE. FROM THEIR BEDROOM WINDOW MARTINA COULD SEE FRUIT TREES THAT HAD ONCE BELONGED TO THE FAMILY. SHE TOOK PRIDE IN STEALING APPLES FROM THOSE TREES, EXPLAINING LATER: "I FELT THE APPLES WERE PART OF MY HERITAGE".

ENCOURAGED IN HER TENNIS BY HER STEPFATHER, MIROSLAV NAVRATIL, SHE RAPIDLY DEVELOPED A POWERFUL, ATTACKING, LEFT-HANDED SERVE-AND-VOLLEY STYLE AND AT THE AGE OF 16 INSPIRED CZECHOSLOVAKIA TO WIN THE BP CUP AT TORQUAY. IN 1975 SHE LED HER COUNTRY TO VICTORY IN THE FEDERATION CUP, AFTER WHICH SHE ASKED FOR REFUGEE STATUS IN AMERICA DURING THE UNITED STATES OPEN. THIS WAS A COURAGEOUS DECISION FOR A GIRL OF 18 TO MAKE AND AT FIRST SHE STRUGGLED TO FULFIL HER POTENTIAL ON THE PROFESSIONAL CIRCUIT IN AMERICA. SEVERAL FACTORS CONTRIBUTED TO THIS, NOT LEAST AN ACQUIRED TASTE FOR FAST FOOD.

IN A SENSE, THERE HAVE BEEN TWO NAVRATILOVAS. FIRST CAME THE RATHER BUXOM BRUNETTE, STILL PRONE TO PUPPYFAT, WHO WON THE WIMBLEDON SINGLES TITLE IN 1978 AND 1979. THEN CAME THE DIET-CONSCIOUS, STREAMLINED, SELF-ASSURED BOTTLE-BLONDE WEIGHT-TRAINER WHO WON WIMBLEDON IN 1982 AS AN AMERICAN CITIZEN.

HAVING CONQUERED WHATEVER PREJUDICE MAY HAVE BEEN PROVOKED BY HER IRON CURTAIN BACKGROUND, NAVRATILOVA HAS SINCE ENCOUNTERED CONTROVERSY CONCERNING HER PRIVATE LIFE. TO HER ENORMOUS CREDIT, SHE HAS REMAINED A POPULAR FIGURE, HER EXPERTISE WITH A RACKET OUTWEIGHING ALL OTHER CONSIDERATIONS, AND HER LONG, WHOLESOME RIVALRY WITH CHRIS EVERT HAS THROUGH THE YEARS SUSTAINED A LIVELY INTEREST IN THE WOMEN'S GAME.

AT WIMBLEDON, ESPECIALLY, THE CROWDS HAVE WARMED PERCEPTIBLY TO THIS GREAT CHAMPION IN RECENT YEARS, AS IF FORSAKING A NATURAL BIAS TOWARDS LESS STURDY PROTAGONISTS, OR PERHAPS REALISING THAT EVEN THE MIGHTY NAVRATILOVA IS VULNERABLE TO SELF-DOUBT. SHE HAS EARNED THE RESPECT AND AFFECTION DUE TO A PLAYER WHO WINS THE WIMBLEDON SINGLES TITLE ON EIGHT OCCASIONS, AND A RECORD SIX TIMES CONSECUTIVELY.

JOHN ROBERTS, THE INDEPENDENT

A DECADE OF DOMINANCE. FAR LEFT – WIMBLEDON, 1977. PHOTOGRAPH BY TONY DUFFY. LEFT – PARIS, 1987. PHOTOGRAPH BY YANN ARTHUS BERTRAND. ABOVE – WIMBLEDON, 1987. PHOTOGRAPH BY CHRIS COLE.

SKY-WALKING BY DOUG LEWIS OF THE UNITED
STATES (ABOVE) AT THE 1987 MEN'S DOWNHILL
WORLD CHAMPIONSHIPS, CRANS MONTANA,
SWITZERLAND. PHOTOGRAPH BY STEVE POWELL.
BY ONE MAN AND HIS DOG (BELOW), SKI-SURFING
AT TIGNES IN THE FRENCH ALPS.
PHOTOGRAPH BY JEAN-MARC BAREY.
AND BY AMERICA'S JAN BUCHER (RIGHT) DURING
THE 1986 FREESTYLE SKIING WORLD
CHAMPIONSHIPS AT TIGNES.
PHOTOGRAPH BY BOB MARTIN.

PERFECT.
WITH TIME RUNNING
AWAY FROM COVENTRY,
TRAILING 2-1 TO SPURS IN
THE 1987 FA CUP FINAL,
KEITH HOUCHEN DIVES,
CONNECTS AND DRAGS THE
UNDERDOGS LEVEL. SPURS
DEFENDER CHRIS HUGHTON
(SECOND RIGHT) IS CLOSE
TO BREAKING POINT. SOON
HIS TEAM-MATE GARY
MABBUTT (THIRD RIGHT)
WAS TO UNDERSTAND THE
PAIN. HIS OWN-GOAL WAS
ENOUGH TO COMPLETE
COVENTRY'S ECSTASY AND
TOTTENHAM'S MISERY.
PHOTOGRAPH BY
DAVID CANNON.

LIKE THE WIND. CARL LEWIS (LEFT), THE ATHLETIC EMBODIMENT OF PERFECT TECHNIQUE AND IRRESISTIBLE POWER, APPROACHES TAKE-OFF SPEED FOR HIS GOLD MEDAL WINNING LONG JUMP AT THE 1984 LOS ANGELES OLYMPICS. HE ALSO WON GOLD IN 4x100 METRES, 200 METRES AND 100 METRES, TO EQUAL JESSE OWENS' ACHIEVEMENT AT THE 1936 BERLIN GAMES – FOUR TRACK GOLDS.
PHOTOGRAPH BY DAVID CANNON.
VALERI BORZOV (RIGHT) FIRES HIMSELF FROM THE BLOCKS LIKE A BULLET FROM A GUN. HIS TARGET WAS 100 METRES GOLD AT THE 1972 MUNICH OLYMPICS. HIS AIM WAS TRUE. PHOTOGRAPH BY DON MORLEY.

DAVID GOWER (LEFT), CALM IN THE STORM OF LEADING ENGLAND DURING
THEIR 5-0 ANNIHILATION BY WEST INDIES – WINTER 1985/86 – A TOUR BESET BY
PROBLEMS ON AND OFF THE FIELD. BY THE MIDDLE OF THE FOLLOWING SUMMER,
AFTER FURTHER TEST DEFEAT BY INDIA, HE HAD BEEN REPLACED BY MIKE GATTING.
PHOTOGRAPH BY ADRIAN MURRELL.

IN 1984, DURING THE FOURTH TEST MATCH AGAINST WEST INDIES AT OLD
TRAFFORD, PAUL TERRY (ABOVE) DISPLAYS COURAGE ABOVE AND BEYOND THE
CALL AGAINST JOEL GARNER. GARNER'S TEAM-MATE, MALCOLM MARSHALL,
WHOSE BOUNCER HOSPITALISED ENGLAND OPENER ANDY LLOYD IN THE FIRST
TEST AND MADE SURE HE PLAYED NO FURTHER PART IN THE SERIES, HAD BROKEN
TERRY'S ARM. BUT NOT HIS SPIRIT. PHOTOGRAPH BY ADRIAN MURRELL.

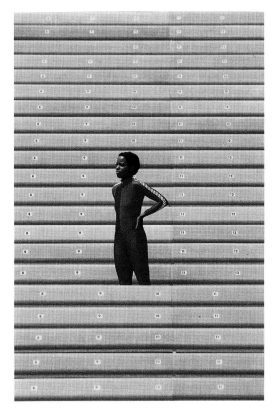

AFTER – THE UNITED STATES 4x100 METRES
SWIMMING TEAM (LEFT) CELEBRATE THE PRIZE OF
OLYMPIC GOLD IN LOS ANGELES, 1984.
PHOTOGRAPH BY TONY DUFFY.
BEFORE – AMERICA'S EVELYN ASHFORD (ABOVE)
DURING TRAINING AT UCLA IN APRIL, 1981. THREE
YEARS LATER, IN THE LOS ANGELES OLYMPICS WOMEN'S
100 METRES, SHE KNEW THE FEELING OF BECOMING A
CHAMPION. PHOTOGRAPH BY TONY DUFFY.

HELD IN FLIGHT BY THE CAMERA, THE CALIFORNIAN SKATEBOARDER (ABOVE).
PHOTOGRAPH BY TONY DUFFY. **THE GRANDEUR AND THE DANGER OF BECHER'S
BROOK, GRAND NATIONAL COURSE, AINTREE (RIGHT).**
PHOTOGRAPH BY MIKE POWELL.

COMBATANTS AND JUDGES, TRANSFIXED BY TENSION.
LOS ANGELES OLYMPICS, 1984. PHOTOGRAPH BY TREVOR JONES.

IT IS A TREMBLING, HEART RACING FEELING, LIKE THE FIRST RUSH OF A TEENAGE CRUSH. EXCITEMENT TINGED WITH DANGER, RIDING THE EDGE OF ANTI-CLIMAX. IT IS THE FEELING YOU GET WHEN IAN BOTHAM IS BATTING FREELY – HEAVING, STRAINING, CONNECTING, DESTROYING – A FEELING WHICH OBLITERATES EVERYTHING ELSE FROM YOUR CONSCIOUSNESS; WATCHING THE PERFECT EXPRESSION OF AGGRESSION.

HEADINGLY, 1981. ENGLAND ARE LOSING THE ASHES SERIES AGAINST AUSTRALIA BY ONE TEST TO NIL. FACING SECOND DEFEAT ON THE FOURTH DAY OF THE MATCH, 135 FOR SEVEN, NO CHANCE.

BOTHAM SMACKS A FEW OVER THE SLIPS, CRACKS A FEW THROUGH THE COVERS. SLOWLY, IMPERCEPTIBLY, HE GROWS IN CONFIDENCE. NOTHING TO LOSE. WHAT THE HELL, SCORES 149 INSPIRED RUNS. STILL AUSTRALIA NEED ONLY 130. BUT, SHELL-SHOCKED AND UNNERVED, CAPITULATE TO BRILLIANT BOWLING BY BOB WILLIS. ENGLAND WIN THE UNWINNABLE TEST AND LATER, AFTER FIVE BOTHAM WICKETS AT EDGBASTON, ANOTHER CENTURY AT OLD TRAFFORD, CONSIDERED ONE OF THE GREATEST EVER SEEN, AND MORE GRUNTING GLORY FROM WILLIS, THE UNWINNABLE SERIES.

STOP THE STORY THERE AND YOU HAVE THE COMPLETE, INVINCIBLE AND UNTARNISHED BOTHAM. GREAT CRICKETER, HUGE PERSONALITY, UNSHAKABLE CONFIDENCE. FURTHERMORE, HIS WALKS TO RAISE MONEY FOR LEUKAEMIA-STRICKEN CHILDREN – 35 PAIN-FILLED DAYS FROM JOHN O' GROATS TO LAND'S END, AND RETRACING THE FOOTSTEPS OF HANNIBAL ACROSS THE ALPS, HAVE MADE HIM KING IN COUNTRIES WHERE CRICKET IS A BIZARRE AND DISTANT RITUAL ENACTED DURING PAUSES BETWEEN THE RAIN SHOWERS OF AN ENGLISH SUMMER.

AND YET … TROUBLE WITH THE LAW, TROUBLE WITH CRICKET AUTHORITIES. BANNED BY ENGLAND, SACKED BY SOMERSET, THROWN OUT OF QUEENSLAND. WILL THE REAL BOTHAM PLEASE STAND UP? ACCORDING TO FRANK KEATING IN HIS VERY PERSONAL STUDY "HIGH, WIDE AND HANDSOME": "HE DRIVES TOO FAST AND, SOMETIMES, DRINKS TOO FAST. HE CAN LIVE VERY DANGEROUSLY INDEED. WARTS AN' ALL … AND QUITE RIGHT TOO. WHEN MORALISTS TALK OF THE NECESSITY FOR 'CHARACTER' IN A MAN THESE DAYS, MORE OFTEN THAN NOT THEY MEAN DULL CHARACTER".

OR IS HE THE GROWN-UP VERSION OF THE TWO-YEAR-OLD IAN BOTHAM WHO, DURING A RUNNING RACE WITH HIS PEERS, STOPPED ONCE HE HAD REACHED THE FRONT, TURNED AND KNOCKED DOWN ALL THE OTHER KIDS ONE BY ONE BEFORE FINISHING THE RACE ON HIS OWN?

IN CRICKETING TERMS, ONE THING IS CERTAIN: BOTHAM IS THE GIANT OF THE MODERN GAME. AS A BATSMAN, HE HITS THE BALL AS THOUGH HE NEVER WANTS TO SEE IT AGAIN. AS A BOWLER, BEARING IN MIND THE NUMBER OF WICKETS TAKEN WITH WHAT HE CALLS "CRAP BALLS", HE CAN GET PEOPLE OUT THROUGH SHEER PRESENCE. AS A FIELDER, HE IS THE ORIGINAL "DID YOU SEE THAT?"

AND YET … IN HIS PERIODIC EXCESSES, BOTHAM CAN LEAVE PEOPLE WHO HAVE NEVER MET HIM WITH THE EMPTY FEELING IN THE PIT OF THE STOMACH OF SOMEONE WHO HAS BEEN LET DOWN, PERSONALLY, BY A FRIEND. IS THE TRUE ANSWER SIMPLY, AS JOHN ARLOTT SUGGESTS, THAT WE ALL REQUIRE TOO MUCH?: "IT'S INCREDIBLE TO ME," HE SAYS, "WE EXPECT THIS CHAP BOTHAM TO WORK CRICKETING MIRACLES EVERY DAY AND STILL BEHAVE LIKE A SOMBRE VEGETABLE – WELL, YOU JUST CAN'T EXPECT THAT, THE TWO THINGS JUST DON'T GO TOGETHER". **PETER HAYTER** ALLSPORT

BOTHAM – A STUDY OF FRUSTRATION (ABOVE) AND A PICTURE OF DEFIANCE (RIGHT). PHOTOGRAPHS BY ADRIAN MURRELL.

CONCENTRATION AND CELEBRATION. ASH LAWRENCE (USA) HOLDS
THE MOMENT (ABOVE). PHOTOGRAPH BY TONY DUFFY.
THE DIVER AND THE DIVE (RIGHT). WENDY WYLAND (USA) STRETCHES FOR
PERFECTION AT MISSION BAY. PHOTOGRAPH BY BOB MARTIN.

CLIMBING A WALL OF WATER (ABOVE) AT THE 1987 WORLD
KAYAK CHAMPIONSHIPS, BOURG ST. MAURICE, FRANCE.
PHOTOGRAPH BY BOB MARTIN.
**JOE BROWN (RIGHT) CLIMBS THE LEFT WALL OF CENOTAPH CORNER,
LLANBERIS PASS, NORTH WALES.** PHOTOGRAPH BY STEVE POWELL.

RESISTIBLE FORCE VERSUS MOVEABLE OBJECTS – THE ESSENTIAL BONE-AND-MUSCLE CONFRONTATION OF AMERICAN FOOTBALL. **USC** V NOTRE DAME AT LOS ANGELES COLISEUM, 1985 (ABOVE) AND THE LOS ANGELES RAIDERS V NEW YORK GIANTS AT ANAHEIM STADIUM, LOS ANGELES, 1984 (RIGHT). PHOTOGRAPHS BY TONY DUFFY.

LOVING CARE. THE RELATIONSHIP BETWEEN A GROUNDSMAN AND HIS CRICKET PITCH CAN BE ALL-CONSUMING. IT INVOLVES SWEEPING THE DUST FROM THE SACRED AND SUN-SCORCHED TURF IN CALCUTTA, INDIA...

...OR IRONING OUT THE LAST WRINKLES IN FAISALABAD, PAKISTAN. TILL DEATH DO THEY PART. PHOTOGRAPHS BY ADRIAN MURRELL.

ANDREJZ KOMAR, OF POLAND (ABOVE), AIRBORNE BY THE SURGE OF
SUCCESS AT THE 1983 WORLD WEIGHTLIFTING CHAMPIONSHIP IN MOSCOW.
PHOTOGRAPH BY STEVE POWELL.
PATRIK SJOBERG, OF SWEDEN (RIGHT) HAS SET A NEW WORLD HIGH JUMP
RECORD – 2.42 METRES/7FT 11¼ INS – IN STOCKHOLM, 1987.
PHOTOGRAPH BY BOB MARTIN.

GENIUS IN PARADISE. VIVIAN RICHARDS (ABOVE) AT HOME IN ANTIGUA DURING HIS WEST INDIES TEAM'S 5-0 THRASHING OF ENGLAND IN 1986. AND AT PEACE. PHOTOGRAPH BY ADRIAN MURRELL.

WHITE BALLS, BLACK SIGHTSCREENS AND COLOURED CLOTHING WERE BY-PRODUCTS OF THE EXPLOSION OF ONE-DAY CRICKET WHICH DOMINATED THE DEVELOPMENT OF THE GAME DURING THE 1970S AND 80S. MICHAEL HOLDING, OF THE WEST INDIES (RIGHT), BOWLS TO ENGLAND CAPTAIN MIKE BREARLEY AT THE SYDNEY CRICKET GROUND IN 1979 DURING ONE OF THE FIRST DAY-NIGHT MATCHES UNDER FLOODLIGHT OFFICIALLY SANCTIONED BY THE WORLD GOVERNING BODIES.

"IT MAY BE CRICKET BUT IS IT CRICKET?" ASKED THE PURISTS. WHATEVER THE ANSWER, HUGE AUDIENCES MADE SURE IT WAS HERE TO STAY. PHOTOGRAPH BY ADRIAN MURRELL.

FIRST THERE IS THE SOUND. IT STARTS AS A WHISPER OF HOT BREATH CUTTING THROUGH A FROSTY MORNING AND WITHIN MOMENTS, GROWS THROUGH A THUNDERING CRESCENDO TO A ROAR. THEN THERE IS THE SIGHT (LEFT), AS 18,000 COMPETITORS IN THE ENGADIN CROSS-COUNTRY SKI MARATHON, NEAR ST. MORITZ, COVER THE FROZEN LAKE LIKE A VAST, BLACK SNAKE. PHOTOGRAPH BY STEVE POWELL. STARBURST (ABOVE) OF THE CHARGE ACROSS THE OCEAN AT THE 1979 COWES–TORQUAY–COWES OFFSHORE POWERBOAT RACE. PHOTOGRAPH BY STEVE POWELL.

KENNY DALGLISH (LEFT) CELEBRATES AFTER
SCORING FOR LIVERPOOL AT ARSENAL ON THE WAY TO
ANOTHER LEAGUE CHAMPIONSHIP IN 1984.
PHOTOGRAPH BY TREVOR JONES.
LIVERPOOL SUPPORTERS (RIGHT) – FAITHFUL SUBJECTS AT
THE COURT OF KING KENNY.
PHOTOGRAPH BY DAVID CANNON.

MAKING HIS WAY TO THE DRESSING ROOM AT WEMBLEY STADIUM IN MAY 1986, AFTER LIVERPOOL HAD COMPLETED THE DOUBLE OF LEAGUE CHAMPIONSHIP AND FA CUP IN HIS FIRST SEASON AS PLAYER-MANAGER, KENNY DALGLISH WAS REQUIRED TO CONSIDER THE FUTURE. "WHERE," HE WAS ASKED, BREATHLESSLY, "DO YOU GO FROM HERE?" DALGLISH DOES NOT SCORN SUCH OPPORTUNITIES. "WELL," HE REPLIED, BUILDING UP TO MISCHIEF. "WE'RE GOING TO HAVE A BATH AND THEN HOME FOR THE BEST PARTY MERSEYSIDE HAS EVER SEEN." END INTERVIEW.

CONVERSATIONS WITH A MAN WHO HAS BEEN DESCRIBED BY HIS PREDECESSOR, BOB PAISLEY, AS THE GREATEST PLAYER IN LIVERPOOL'S HISTORY, EVOKE A SENSE OF WHAT IT MUST HAVE BEEN LIKE TO DEFEND AGAINST HIM. THE VERBAL MANOEUVRES ARE DISCONCERTINGLY ADROIT AND MERCILESSLY FLAT-FOOTING. "KENNY, HOW DID YOU SEE THE PENALTY?"… "FROM THE DUG-OUT."

CAST SIGNIFICANTLY IN THE MOULD OF BILL SHANKLY, THE LEGENDARY MANAGER WHOSE TENETS REMAIN CENTRAL TO THE ACHIEVEMENTS THAT HAVE ESTABLISHED LIVERPOOL AS THE MOST CONSISTENTLY EFFECTIVE FORCE BRITISH FOOTBALL HAS EVER KNOWN, DALGLISH EMBODIES ALL THE QUALITIES ASSOCIATED WITH ANFIELD: COMMITMENT, UNSWERVING LOYALTY AND THE PURSUIT OF EXCELLENCE.

ARTHUR HOPCRAFT'S SPLENDID BOOK, THE FOOTBALL MAN, PUBLISHED IN 1968 BEFORE SUPPORTERS OF CELTIC WERE FULLY AWARE THAT A PRODIGIOUS TALENT HAD ARRIVED IN THEIR MIDST, CONTAINS THIS PERCEPTIVE REFERENCE TO FOOTBALL MANAGEMENT: "IN THE END HE IS THE SUM OF HIS RESULTS, AND HIS PROBLEM IS THAT, WHILE HE CAN DEVELOP PLAYERS, BUY TALENT, DRIVE AND COAX AND PLAN, HE IS POWERLESS DURING THE GAME. DISAFFECTED PLAYERS CAN RUIN HIM, UNLESS HE CAN CONVINCE DIRECTORS OF HIS PARAMOUNT IMPORTANCE." PLENTY OF OUTSTANDING PLAYERS HAVE FLINCHED FROM THOSE HAZARDS BUT NOT DALGLISH, WHO BECAME LIVERPOOL'S MANAGER THE MORNING AFTER THE WORST DAY THEY HAVE EVER EXPERIENCED, AN OUTBREAK OF HOOLIGANISM DURING THE EUROPEAN CUP FINAL WITH JUVENTUS AT THE HEYSEL STADIUM IN BRUSSELS ON MAY 29, 1985, RESULTING IN SLAUGHTER AND INFAMY. NOTHING COULD OBLITERATE THE HORROR, BUT WITHIN A YEAR DALGLISH HAD DONE MUCH TO RESTORE LIVERPOOL'S REPUTATION, THE TRANSITION FROM CELEBRATED PLAYER TO SUCCESSFUL MANAGER ACCOMPLISHED SO SMOOTHLY THAT HE WAS STILL ABLE TO PLAY A DECISIVE ROLE ON THE FIELD.

WHEN SECURING ANOTHER CHAMPIONSHIP WITH A GOAL AGAINST CHELSEA ON MAY 3, 1986, DALGLISH FURTHER EMPHASISED THE EXTENT OF GIFTS THAT HAVE BEEN EMPLOYED SO MARVELLOUSLY IN THE COLOURS OF CELTIC, LIVERPOOL AND SCOTLAND. THE ULTIMATE TRIBUTE WILL ALWAYS BE THE AWE HE INSPIRES IN FELLOW PROFESSIONALS, AMONG THEM GRAEME SOUNESS, WHO INSISTS HE HAS NOT SEEN A BETTER ALL-ROUND PLAYER.

DALGLISH HAS NEVER POSSESSED THE PACE NORMALLY ASSOCIATED WITH GREAT GOALSCORERS BUT, AS THE LATE JOCK STEIN ONCE SAID: "WHEN DID FERENC PUSKAS EVER RUN PAST ANYBODY?" **KEN JONES** THE INDEPENDENT

INGENUITY IN MOTION. THE HARNESSING OF USABLE NATURAL ENERGY HAS BEEN A CONSTANT THROUGHOUT MAN'S TECHNOLOGICAL DEVELOPMENT. BALLOONING (ABOVE), AS AT ASHTON COURT, BRISTOL, IN 1987, REPRESENTED THE FIRST FORM OF AIR TRANS-PORT (ICARUS NOTWITHSTANDING), AND REMAINS THE MOST AESTHETIC. PHOTOGRAPH BY OLI TENNANT.

AND NOW, ON THE 2,000 MILE STUART HIGHWAY FROM DARWIN TO ADELAIDE THROUGH THE RED-HOT CENTRE OF AUSTRALIA, COMES "SUNRAYCER" (RIGHT), COURTESY OF A 15 MILLION DOLLAR PROJECT BY GENERAL MOTORS TO DESIGN AND BUILD A SOLAR POWERED CAR TO WIN THE 1987 PENTAX WORLD SOLAR CHALLENGE RACE. TRAVELLING AT AN AVERAGE SPEED OF 55 KPH, IT DID – BY TWO DAYS.

PHOTOGRAPH BY SIMON BRUTY.

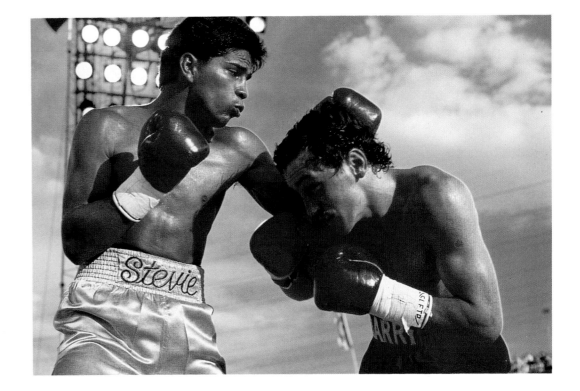

TELEVISION REVENUES MADE FIGHTING IN THE HEAT OF LAS VEGAS AN OFFER IRELAND'S
BARRY MCGUIGAN (ABOVE) COULDN'T REFUSE. AGAINST STEVE CRUZ HE PAID THE PRICE, LOSING HIS
WORLD FEATHERWEIGHT TITLE IN 1986, FINISHING IN A STATE OF NEAR-EXHAUSTION.
PHOTOGRAPH BY MIKE POWELL.
THE PRESENCE OF THE CAMERAS ALSO ATTRACTS THE SPONSOR'S EYE FOR THE MAIN CHANCE (LEFT)
PHOTOGRAPH BY MIKE POWELL.

MEN AND MACHINE. DENNIS IRELAND
(ABOVE) TRIES TO SHUT OFF THE THROTTLE BEFORE
LOSING CONTROL OF HIS 500CC MOTORCYCLE,
DEMOLISHING A CONCRETE POST AND BREAKING HIS
THIGHBONE. PHOTOGRAPH BY DON MORLEY.
RANDY MAMOLA (RIGHT) SHAKES A LEG AS HE
TAKES A CORNER IN THE 1984 TRANSATLANTIC
CHALLENGE AT DONINGTON.
PHOTOGRAPH BY BOB MARTIN.

AURELIA DOBRÉ, OF ROMANIA, 1987 WORLD GYMNASTICS CHAMPIONSHIPS, ROTTERDAM.

PHOTOGRAPH BY BOB MARTIN.

OLGA KORBUT, THE GREAT RUSSIAN OLYMPIC AND WORLD CHAMPION, IN EXHIBITION, 1973.

PHOTOGRAPH BY TONY DUFFY.

"WE REGRET TO ANNOUNCE" ... FLOOD STOPS PLAY AT
WIMBLEDON, 1985 (ABOVE). PHOTOGRAPH BY STEVE POWELL.
WINDSURFER GREG AGUERA (LEFT) RIDES THE TIDAL
TEMPEST IN HAWAII. PHOTOGRAPH BY CHRISTIAN LE BOZEC.

BACKSTROKE. 1987 EUROPEAN CHAMPIONSHIPS, STRASBOURG. PHOTOGRAPH BY SIMON BRUTY.

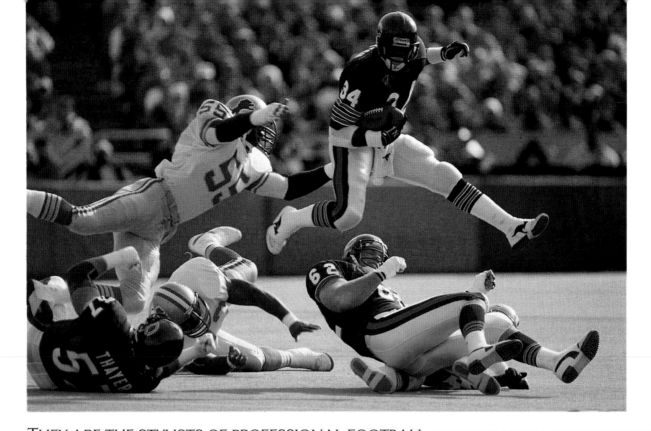

WALTER PAYTON (LEFT) RUSHING FOR CHICAGO IN HIS LAST REGULAR-SEASON HOME GAME, AGAINST THE DETROIT LIONS. PHOTOGRAPH BY TONY INZERILLO. AND (RIGHT) REFLECTING ON THE END OF THE LONG RUN. PHOTOGRAPH BY MIKE POWELL.

THEY ARE THE STYLISTS OF PROFESSIONAL FOOTBALL, THE ARTISTS. NAME A GREAT RUNNING BACK AND YOU WILL RECALL HIS OWN INDIVIDUAL BRUSH STROKE, HIS OWN GRACE NOTE. COACHES LEARN NOT TO MESS WITH THEIR TALENTS, NOT TO TAKE AWAY THAT SIGNATURE. THE VISIONS COME FLOODING BACK. LARRY CSONKA – A WRECKER'S BALL KNOCKING DOWN A WALL. JIM BROWN – POWER AND GRACE, A LION ON THE HUNT. GALE SAYERS – A WISP OF SMOKE. O.J. SIMPSON – A SURGEON'S PROBE, THE GLIDE AND THEN THE QUICK INCISION. AND WHAT OF WALTER PAYTON, WHO CARRIED THE BALL MORE TIMES FOR MORE YARDS THAN ANY MAN IN HISTORY? WHAT ARE THE MEMORIES OF WALTER? CONTROLLED FURY. HE PLAYED EACH GAME IN A KIND OF RAGE, WAGING A WAR AGAINST EACH INDIVIDUAL TACKLER.

HE DID IT AGAIN AND AGAIN. HE DID IT ON HOPELESS CHICAGO BEAR TEAMS THAT HAD LITTLE ELSE, HE SUFFERED THROUGH A DREARY COLLECTION OF QUARTERBACKS, UNTIL JIM MCMAHON FINALLY ARRIVED IN THE EIGHTH OF PAYTON'S 13-YEAR CAREER. HE PLAYED WITH BROKEN RIBS AND NERVE DAMAGE SO SEVERE THAT HE COULDN'T RAISE HIS RIGHT ARM ABOVE SHOULDER LEVEL. HE MISSED ONE GAME IN 13 YEARS.

WHAT DO I REMEMBER OF WALTER? I REMEMBER THE FIRST TIME HE GOT INTO THE PLAYOFFS – AGAINST DALLAS IN 1977 – AND HE CAUGHT A LITTLE SWING PASS, AND JUST AS HE TURNED UPFIELD CLIFF HARRIS, THE FREE SAFETY, CLOSED IN FOR THE KILL. HARRIS, WIRY, EXPLOSIVE, A FEROCIOUS HITTER … TEXAS COACH DARRELL ROYAL ONCE CALLED HIM, "A ROLLING BALL OF BUTCHER'S KNIVES" … HAD THE MOMENTUM, AND THE ANGLE, A COMBINATION THAT HAD LEFT A TRAIL OF UNCONSCIOUS BALL CARRIERS THROUGHOUT THE NFL. HE LEVELLED THE FULL POWER OF HIS KILLER SHOT ON PAYTON, HEAD HIGH, AND WALTER TOOK THE BLOW, BOUNCED UP, TAPPED HARRIS ONCE ON THE BACKSIDE WITH THE BALL AND JOGGED BACK TO THE HUDDLE. "DID YOU SEE THAT?" HARRIS SAID AFTERWARD. WHAT'S THAT GUY MADE OF, ANYWAY?" MUSCLE, WIRES, SPARKS, FLAME, RAGE, YES THAT WAS THE KEY TO IT. HE ATTACKED THE TACKLERS.

MEMORIES OF WALTER. WE ARE IN THE LOUNGE OF ONE OF THE PLAYERS' DORMITORIES IN LAKE FOREST, ILL., IN THE SUMMER OF 1982. WALTER HAS BROUGHT HIS MOTORCYCLE INSIDE, AND AS WE TALK HE STARES AT IT. HE IS IN LOVE WITH MOTION, WITH SPEED. HE BOUNCES UP OFF HIS CHAIR. HE TAPS THE MOTORCYCLE, BOUNCES ON THE SEAT, HOPS OFF, TRIES A MOCK CHARGE AT THE WALL, TAPS IT, WHEELS, FACES ME AND STANDS THERE, BOUNCING LIGHTLY ON THE BALLS OF HIS FEET, NEVER LOSING THE THREAD OF THE INTERVIEW. HE CAN'T BE STILL. UNCONTROLLABLE ENERGY. IN THE DIM LIGHT HE LOOKS ALMOST LUMINESCENT. HIS EYES FLASH. HE APPEARS TO BE ON FIRE.

HE IS TALKING OF HIS TRAINING METHODS, RUNNING THE LEVEE, A BRUTAL 45-DEGREE SLOPE BY THE PEARL RIVER IN MISSISSIPPI, 15 TIMES, 20 TIMES, "UNTIL YOUR THIGHS BURN," HE SAYS. HE TALKS ABOUT OTHER ATHLETES WHO TRIED TO RUN IT WITH HIM, HOW HE BURNED THEM OUT ONE BY ONE. A QUICK SMILE, THE FLASHING EYES. EVERYTHING IN STACCATO BURSTS. A 5FT 10½IN, 204-POUND PACKAGE OF RAW ENERGY THAT TRULY WAS CREATED FOR THE GAME OF FOOTBALL. IN 1981 HE SIGNED THE RICHEST CONTRACT IN THE NFL. JIM FINKS, THE BEARS' GENERAL MANAGER, WAS ASKED IF THIS WEREN'T PERHAPS A TRIFLE EXTRAVAGANT FOR A TEAM KNOWN FOR ITS FRUGALITY. "FOR ANOTHER PLAYER, MAYBE," HE SAID, "BUT WALTER'S GOT THE SKINS ON THE WALL."

PAUL ZIMMERMAN SPORTS ILLUSTRATED

THE BEAUTY OF THE ICE-DANCE. SRETENSKI AND ANNENKO, OF THE SOVIET UNION (LEFT), AT THE MOMENT WHICH TRANSCENDS MERE SPORT. 1988 CALGARY WINTER OLYMPICS. PHOTOGRAPH BY DAVID CANNON. PAUL WYLIE (ABOVE) SKATES THE EDGE. PHOTOGRAPH BY RUSSELL CHEYNE.

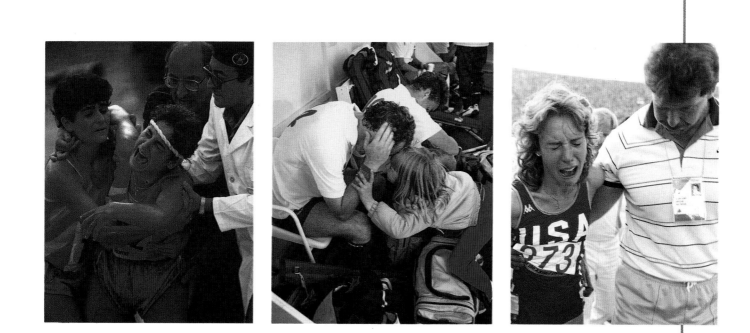

COLLISION: Nakatake, of Japan (left), tangles with Lee, of Taiwan, during the **1984** Los Angeles Olympics. Photograph by David Cannon.

COLLAPSE: Emilia Cano, of Spain (above left), physically destroyed after finishing **29**th in the **10**km walk at the Rome World Championships. Photograph by Bob Martin.

COMFORT: Norman Hughes, of England (above centre), is taken in hand by his daughter after losing to Australia in the final of the **1986** World Hockey Cup. Photograph by Simon Bruty.

INCONSOLABLE: Mary Decker (above right) led away, distraught, by future husband Richard Slaney after her accidental clash with Zola Budd and consequent withdrawal from the **3000**metres final at the Los Angeles Olympics. Photograph by Tony Duffy.

AFTER THE BURN-UP, DAVE MILLER (ABOVE) EXECUTES A PERFECT TAKE-OFF AT POMOMA, CALIFORNIA, IN HIS TOP FUEL DRAGSTER, THE FORMULA ONE OF DRAG

RACING. PHOTOGRAPH BY MIKE POWELL.

ELSEWHERE IN THE CALIFORNIAN DESERT (RIGHT), THE SHEER SANDY CHAOS OF FOUR-WHEEL MOTORBIKES – QUAD RACING. PHOTOGRAPH BY MIKE POWELL.

GERHARD BERGER, OF AUSTRIA. SUCCESSIVE 1987 GRAND PRIX WINS IN
JAPAN AND AUSTRALIA ENGENDERED FERRARI HOPES OF A FORMULA ONE REVIVAL.
HIS SECOND PLACE IN THE FIRST RACE OF 1988 – THE BRAZILIAN GRAND PRIX, RIO DE
JANEIRO (RIGHT) – EMPHASISED THEIR CREDIBILITY. PHOTOGRAPH BY SIMON BRUTY.

STRETCHING A POINT. RIC CHARLESWORTH (ABOVE), CAPTAIN OF THE AUSTRALIAN HOCKEY TEAM, EMPLOYS A NOVEL METHOD TO TACKLE FRIED, OF WEST GERMANY,
AT THE 1986 WORLD CUP. PHOTOGRAPH BY SIMON BRUTY.

RON HARPER (RIGHT), OF THE CLEVELAND CAVALIERS, PREPARES TO SHOOT DURING THE 1987 ALL STAR GAME AT THE LOS ANGELES FORUM. PHOTOGRAPH BY MIKE POWELL.

JUNIOR FINAL, 1987 FRENCH OPEN, ROLAND GARROS STADIUM, PARIS.

PHOTOGRAPH BY YANN ARTHUS BERTRAND.

BULL'S-EYE FOR JOHN LOWE, OF ENGLAND (ABOVE), AS HE PINPOINTS THE
TARGET AT THE **1987** EMBASSY WORLD DARTS CHAMPIONSHIP.
PHOTOGRAPH BY SIMON BRUTY.

TIM HILL (RIGHT), OWNER/DRIVER, POINTS HIS POWERBOAT STRAIGHT AS AN
ARROW AT THE **1986** EUROPEAN CHAMPIONSHIP AT GUERNSEY.
PHOTOGRAPH BY OLI TENNANT.

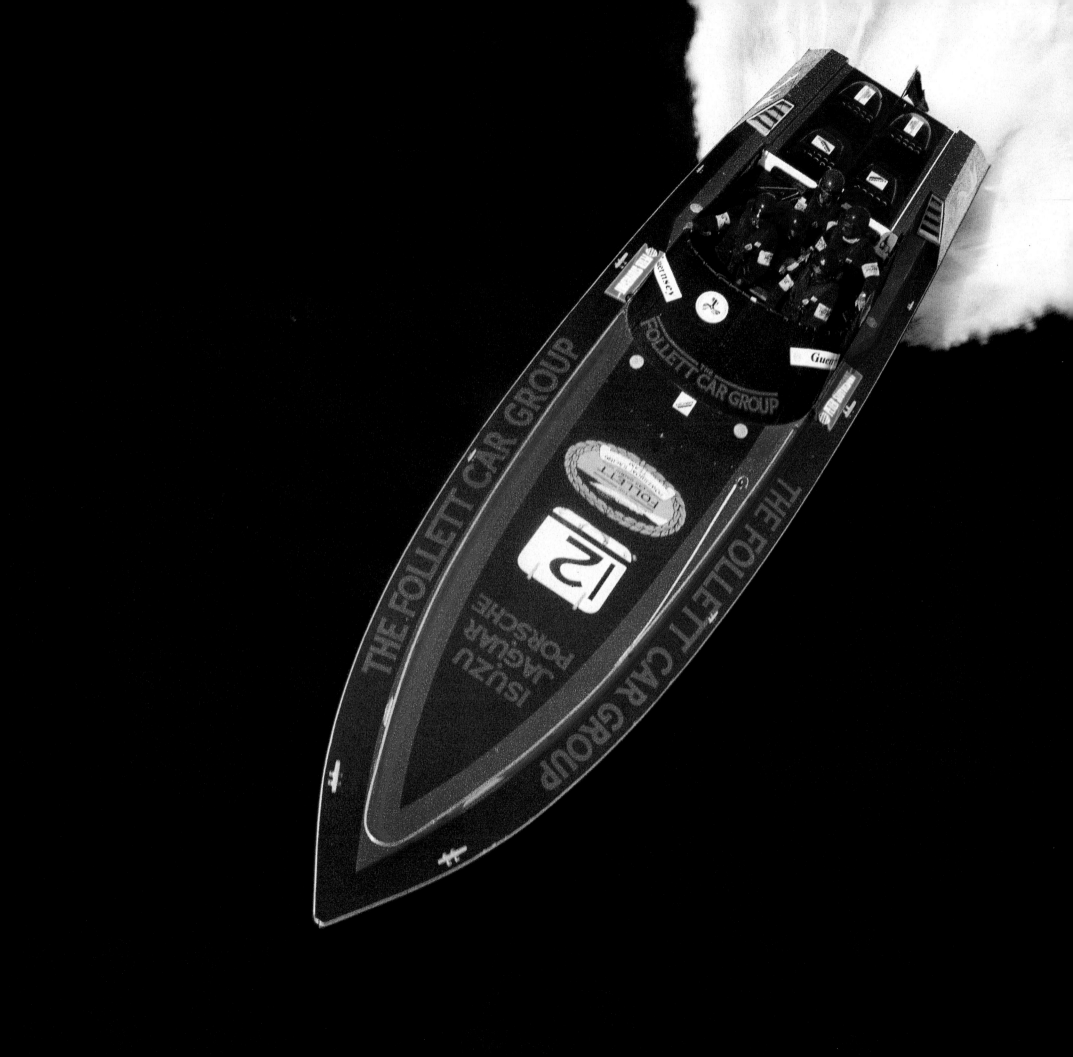

As Jack Nicklaus approaches the end of his distinguished career, two questions should properly be put. Where does he rank among players in the history of the game and, more interestingly, what has been the motor that for years has driven this odd, proud and possessed man?

The wonderful striker-competitor Ben Hogan was probably the finest of all golfers, for starters, so let us deprive Nicklaus of that crown. What is more, let us fudge the incompatibility-of-eras issue and get on with a more common debate: was Nicklaus a greater player than his hero, Bobby Jones? It is a beguiling argument and, in my case, one admittedly weakened by only a slight acquaintanceship with Jones, in the flesh and on film.

At this writing, Nicklaus has won 20 major events, including two US Amateur championships, while Jones, in eight seasons, captured 13 majors, seven of them Opens on either side of the Atlantic. The statistics, therefore, would seem heavily to favour Nicklaus, save for the fact that Jones' seven match-play victories were often sterner psychological examinations. A more useful speculation is whether Nicklaus would beat Jones with wooden-shafted clubs or Jones triumph while wielding the modern, stepped-down metal shafts. End of argument. Given a bit of practice, Jones would win in a walk for no man, even Hogan, hit a ball more sweetly, and no man, even Nicklaus, could rise to such levels of head-to-head combat. Put Nicklaus third in history, then. Unless some Fin de siecle freak makes a case for Harry Vardon or an historian, steeped in romance, for sad young Tom Morris, dead at 24, more than a century ago.

Furthermore, Nicklaus suffers as a performer. It's not his fault. He has been too awesomely efficient, his composure so absolute – his skills so buried in power – that he appears to be a less exciting golfer than many of his contemporaries. Ballesteros, Johnny Miller and even Tony Jacklin come to mind and, most of all, Arnold Palmer. In fact, I'm confident that in that last magic man, Palmer, lies the secret to Nicklaus' relentless drive to the top of the game. The year was 1962, the place Oakmont, Pennsylvania. The occasion was the US Open championship. Palmer, the most deeply worshipped golfer since Jones, was only 32 years old and seemingly at the peak of his career. Nicklaus, 22, and still without a professional victory, was at the outset of his and frankly presented an unattractive, baby-fat figure. He won the title in a play-off.

Nicklaus had killed the King. He was not, perhaps never was, forgiven. In subsequent tournaments the fans treated him with grotesque, unsportsmanlike conduct. Placards were held up beside bunkers reading: "Put it here, Fat Jack." At best, he was ignored. Palmer did little to correct the inattention, divert the cruel fire and Nicklaus never forgot.

To his credit, he prevailed. Fat Jack was to become the Golden Bear, the richest and most successful golfer in history. He also was to become a golf course designer whose trademark has been to bring in the bulldozers, never to leave nature alone. As a player, emphatic and workmanlike, Jack Nicklaus, likewise, has changed the landscape of golf. **DUDLEY DOUST** THE SUNDAY TIMES

JACK NICKLAUS (RIGHT) SANDBLASTING DURING THE 1986 US MASTERS AT AUGUSTA. PHOTOGRAPH BY DAVID CANNON.

118

BLINDING PAIN. MIKE GATTING (LEFT), THE ENGLAND BATSMAN, HAS HIS NOSE SHATTERED
BY MALCOLM MARSHALL, OF WEST INDIES, DURING THE ONE-DAY INTERNATIONAL AT SABINA
PARK, KINGSTON, JAMAICA, 1986. WHEN HE RECOVERED HIS SENSES IT WAS ALSO DISCOVERED
THAT THE BALL HAD BOUNCED INTO THE WICKET FROM HIS FACE. OUT COLD AND OUT, BOWLED.
GATTING RETURNED TO ENGLAND TO RECUPERATE AND BRAVELY REJOINED THE BATTLE IN TIME TO
PREPARE FOR THE THIRD TEST MATCH IN A DISTRICT GAME AGAINST BARBADOS. TWENTY HOURS
AFTER LANDING, HE WAS REWARDED WITH A BROKEN THUMB. PHOTOGRAPH BY ADRIAN MURRELL.
KEEPING YOUR EYES ON THE BALL (ABOVE). PHOTOGRAPH BY JOHN GICHIGI.

LADY TIGER TRIMIAR (ABOVE), AMERICAN WOMAN BOXER.
PHOTOGRAPH BY TONY DUFFY.

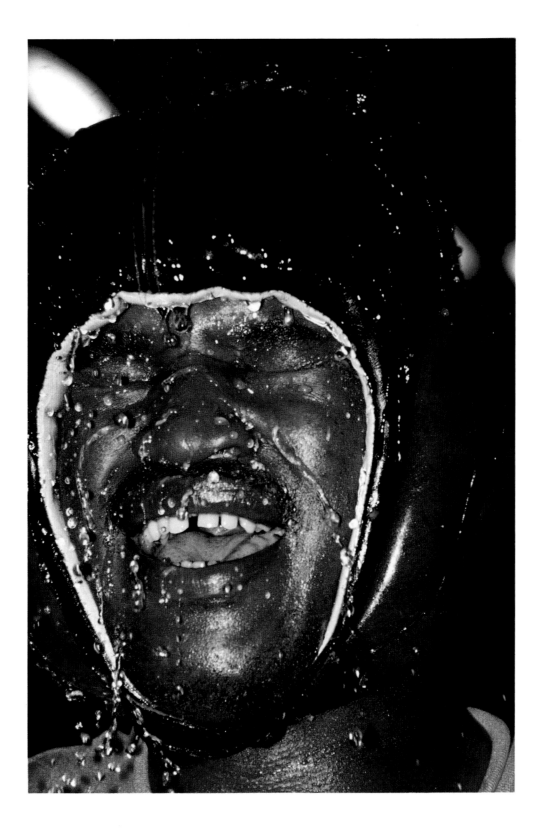

LARRY HOLMES (ABOVE) IN TRAINING FOR HIS WORLD HEAVYWEIGHT TITLE
FIGHT WITH MUHAMMAD ALI IN LAS VEGAS, 1980. TRIUMPH FOR HOLMES, THE
END FOR ALI. PHOTOGRAPH BY STEVE POWELL.

BAREFOOT IN THE PARK. STREAKER AT TWICKENHAM (LEFT)

IS AN ARRESTING SIGHT AT THE ENGLAND VERSUS WALES INTERNATIONAL, 1974.

PHOTOGRAPH BY TONY DUFFY.

CALGARY WINTER OLYMPICS, 1988 (LEFT). MEN'S DOWNHILL.

ASCOT RACES, 1987 (ABOVE). DIAMOND DAY. PHOTOGRAPHS BY PASCAL RONDEAU.

BORIS BECKER, OF WEST GERMANY (RIGHT), DISPLAYS THE DEPTH OF DESIRE THAT MAKES A CHAMPION IN THE **1986** WIMBLEDON FINAL AGAINST IVAN LENDL. PHOTOGRAPH BY STEVE POWELL.
BRYAN ROBSON'S WORLD CUP – MEXICO **1986** – IS OVER (ABOVE). THE ENGLAND CAPTAIN PLAYED IN A HARNESS TO PROTECT HIS SHOULDER INJURY BUT, AGAINST MOROCCO, FELL BADLY. THE ANGUISH ON HIS FACE REVEALS THE TRUTH. HE DID NOT PLAY AGAIN DURING THE TOURNAMENT. PHOTOGRAPH BY DAVID CANNON.

MATS WILANDER, 1987 US OPEN. PHOTOGRAPH BY CHRIS COLE.

THE ROYAL FAMILY APART, YOU WOULD PROBABLY HAVE TO GO BACK TO THE SALAD DAYS OF LAURENCE OLIVIER AND VIVIEN LEIGH TO FIND A PARALLEL TO THE PUBLIC INTEREST GENERATED BY THE PARTNERSHIP OF JAYNE TORVILL AND CHRISTOPHER DEAN DURING THE FOUR YEARS OF THEIR DOMINATION OF ICE DANCING, FROM 1981 TO 1984. BUT WHEREAS THE ACTORS CARRIED THEIR ROMANTIC STAGE AND STUDIO PERSONAE INTO REAL LIFE, THE SKATERS REMAINED MYSTERIOUSLY ENIGMATIC ON THE SUBJECT. "NOT THIS WEEK", WAS THEIR STOCK REPLY TO QUESTIONS ABOUT IMPENDING MARRIAGE. IT WAS HARD TO BELIEVE THAT THEY COULD ACHIEVE SUCH PASSIONATE UNISON ON THE ICE WITHOUT A MATCHING UNION OFF IT.

FOUR YEARS ON, THE AFFINITY SEEMS UNCHANGED, UNSHAKABLY STRONG IN SPITE OF RUMOURS THAT HAVE LINKED THEM SEPARATELY WITH DIFFERENT PARTNERS, IN ONE OR TWO CASES LUDICROUSLY SO. BUT AS TIME MARCHES ON AND THEY LEAVE BEHIND THEIR 30TH BIRTHDAYS THEIR RELATIONSHIP HAS TO BE ACCEPTED ON FACE VALUE, THAT IS RATHER AS BROTHER AND SISTER, THOUGH WITH A DEPTH OF RAPPORT THAT NO SIBLINGS COULD EVER ACHIEVE.

WHATEVER THE MYSTERY OF THEIR PRIVATE LIVES, THERE HAS NEVER BEEN ANY QUESTION ABOUT THEIR CHARACTERS WHEN PRACTISING THEIR ART, EITHER IN THEIR AMATEUR DAYS OR NOW AS PROFESSIONALS. THEY ARE, QUITE SIMPLY, PARALYSINGLY THE BEST, NOT ONLY AMONG THEIR CONTEMPORARIES, BUT ALSO AGAINST THE BACKDROP OF HISTORY. EVEN THE SOVIET UNION, WHO HAVE BEEN SUPREME IN ICE DANCE FOR TWO DECADES EXCEPT FOR THE TORVILL AND DEAN YEARS, HAVE RECENTLY ADMITTED AS MUCH, THROUGH THE WORDS OF ONE OF THEIR TRAINERS DURING THE WINTER OLYMPICS IN CALGARY THIS YEAR .

FROM HUMBLE NOTTINGHAM ORIGINS THEY LEFT SCHOOL TO BECOME A POLICEMAN AND AN INSURANCE CLERK, WITH NOTHING, IT SEEMED, TO SET THEM APART. BUT FROM SOMEWHERE DEEP IN THEIR GENES, GOING BACK GENERATIONS, ARTISTIC INSPIRATION TOUCHED THEM BOTH. DURING THE FOUR YEARS OF THEIR UNCHALLENGED SUPREMACY IN THE AMATEUR FIELD THEY DISPLAYED UNEXPECTED POWERS OF INNOVATION (THE CHOREOGRAPHY WAS MOSTLY THEIR OWN CREATION) AND STUNNING POWERS OF PERFORMANCE. THE CONVENTIONAL FOUR-PART PROGRAMME WHICH WON THEIR FIRST WORLD CHAMPIONSHIP IN THE UNITED STATES IN 1981 WAS SUCCEEDED IN THE FOLLOWING YEARS BY THE GOLDEN GAIETY OF MACK AND MABEL, THE DEMANDING ACROBATICS OF BARNUM AND THE EXQUISITE BEAUTY OF BOLERO.

THEY REACHED THEIR APOTHEOSIS WITH BOLERO AT THE WINTER OLYMPICS OF 1984. UNTIL THEN I HAD ALWAYS REGARDED THE WEMBLEY WORLD CUP FINAL OF 1966 AS THE MOST MEMORABLE MOMENT IN SPORT. BOLERO TRANSCENDED IT IN SARAJEVO AS TORVILL AND DEAN UNCONSCIOUSLY WOVE THEIR MAGIC, UNCONSCIOUSLY BECAUSE THEY SKATED RATHER FOR EACH OTHER THAN FOR NINE MEN AND WOMEN SITTING IN JUDGEMENT AND THE WATCHING MILLIONS ON TELEVISION. THE FOLLOWING DAY THEY COULD RECALL NOTHING BETWEEN THE OPENING AND CLOSING BARS OF RAVEL'S THROBBING MUSIC. THE ESSENCE OF THE PERFORMANCE WAS ENCAPSULATED IN ONE TOUCHING MOMENT WHEN THEY CAME WITHIN A MILLIMETRE OF A KISS ON THE ICE, HE ALL MACHO MASTERFULNESS, SHE ALL MELTING SURRENDER. HOW COULD A GOAL AT WEMBLEY POSSIBLY COMPARE WITH THAT?

JOHN HENNESSY THE TIMES

JAYNE TORVILL AND CHISTOPHER DEAN. BOLERO (ABOVE), SARAJEVO WINTER OLYMPICS, 1984. PHOTOGRAPH BY TREVOR JONES. BARNUM (RIGHT), RICHMOND, 1983. PHOTOGRAPH BY BOB MARTIN.

A MOMENT OF PRIVACY FOR CHRIS EVERT (ABOVE) AT WIMBLEDON, 1982. PHOTOGRAPH BY TONY DUFFY.
TRANQUILITY FOR BRITAIN'S FLY-FISHING TEAM (LEFT), LAKE BLAGDON. PHOTOGRAPH BY ADRIAN MURRELL.

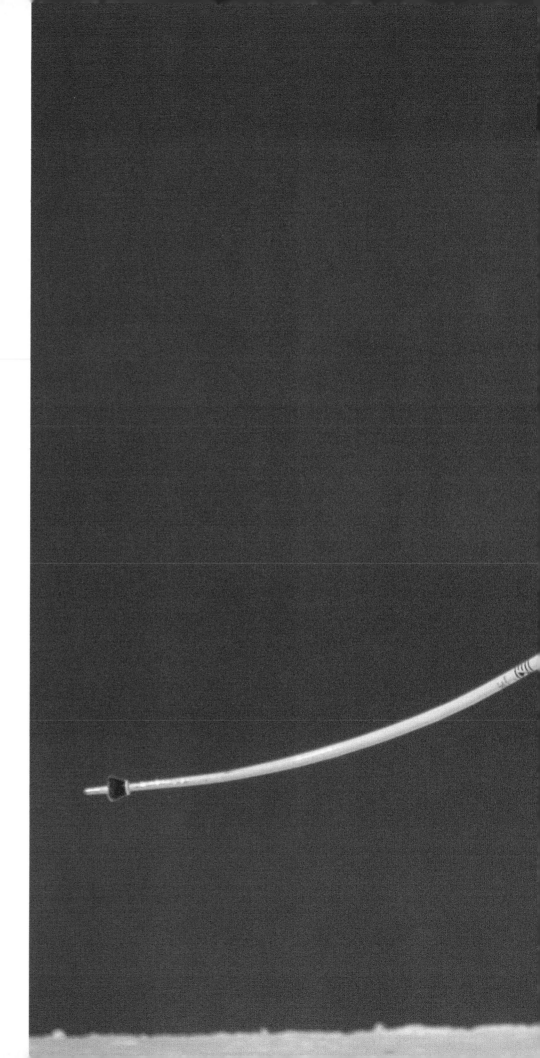

THE PERFECT PRECISION OF PIETRO ALBERTELLI, OF
ITALY (ABOVE), 200 KPH OF POWER ON SKIS AT LES ARCS, 1978.
PHOTOGRAPH BY TONY DUFFY.
THE PERFECT POISE OF WEST GERMAN HANNES ZEHENTNER
(RIGHT) AT THE CALGARY WINTER OLYMPICS 1988.
PHOTOGRAPH BY DAVID CANNON.

THE GUN.
100 METRES HEATS,
LOS ANGELES OLYMPICS, 1984.
PHOTOGRAPH BY TONY DUFFY.

138

IF EVER YOU WANT TO BEAT DALEY THOMPSON AT ANYTHING, SPRING IT ON HIM. CHOOSE YOUR SPORT, THROW DOWN THE CHALLENGE AND GET TO IT. GIVE HIM WARNING AND YOU'RE LOST. HE WILL PRACTICE FOR HOURS. IT WAS THAT WAY WHEN AN ADVERTISING AGENCY ASKED HIM TO SERVE TO A WOODEN CUT-OUT OF AN OPPONENT ACROSS A TENNIS NET FOR A TELEVISION COMMERCIAL. THOMPSON JOINED QUEEN'S CLUB AND TOOK LESSONS FROM THE PROFESSIONAL FOR WEEKS AHEAD OF THE SHOOT.

THOMPSON IS A NATURAL ATHLETE. HE WAS BORN QUICK AND WELL CO-ORDINATED WITH INSTINCTIVE TIMING AND HE OWES THAT TO HIS BLOOD LINES. IN A SENSE, HE WAS BORN LUCKY. THE REST OF IT HAS TAKEN TIME, AND AN INFINITE CAPACITY FOR PRACTISING THE SAME MOVEMENT UNTIL ALL ELEMENTS OF LUCK HAVE BEEN REMOVED. THOMPSON HAS WORKED AT BECOMING THE WORLD'S MOST COMPLETE ATHLETE. IN THAT SENSE, HE IS MAN-MADE, THE PRODUCT OF RELENTLESS REHEARSAL.

THE DECATHLON, MORE THAN ALL SPORTING EVENTS, DEMANDS SUCH COMMITMENT IN GOOD MEASURE. IT IS NOT, AS MANY PERCEIVE, 10 INDEPENDENT ATHLETIC EVENTS BUT ONE, WITH 10 INTER-DEPENDENT PARTS REQUIRING 10 TIMES AS MUCH STUDY. THOMPSON IS NOT A JACK-OF-ALL-TRADES BUT A MASTER OF ONE. FEW WOULD DISAGREE THAT THOMPSON, GIVEN HIS NATURAL ASSETS AND HIS GREAT DETERMINATION, COULD HAVE BEEN AMONG THE WORLD'S FASTEST MEN HAD HE SPECIALISED IN HIS FIRST LOVE OF SPRINTING. OR GONE FAR BEYOND 8.12 METRES IN THE LONG JUMP. AND PROBABLY RUN 400 METRES IN SUB-45 SECONDS. AND HE HAS THE SPEED, CO-ORDINATION AND STRENGTH TO HAVE BEEN A FINE POLE VAULTER.

BUT TO BE THE GREATEST DECATHLETE THE WORLD HAS KNOWN HE HAD TO SACRIFICE THE WEIGHT HE NEEDED FOR THE SHOT TO GAIN A FEW POINTS IN THE HIGH JUMP, THE SPEED HE NEEDED FOR THE DASH FOR THE STAMINA NEEDED FOR 1500 METRES. SPECIFICALLY, HE IS EXPERT AT THE VERY SPECIAL ART OF COMPROMISING ON TIME AND EFFORT ON EACH OF THE PARTS TO ACHIEVE THE WHOLE.

HE CLAIMED ONCE TO ME THAT MOST CHAMPION ATHLETES HE KNEW WERE SELF-CENTRED, SELF-OPINIONATED AND SELF-INDULGENT. "AND SINGLE-MINDEDNESS IS AN ASSET," HE ADDED. TO THOSE WHO KNOW HIM – AND PROBABLY HUNDREDS WHO DON'T – THOMPSON HAS APPEARED AT TIMES TO HAVE ALL OF THOSE QUALITIES, AND WE SHOULD NOT FAULT HIM FOR THAT. HE WOULD NOT BE WHAT HE IS OTHERWISE, AND CAN MANY OF US CLAIM NEVER TO HAVE TAKEN A VICARIOUS DELIGHT IN THAT? CERTAINLY THERE ARE FEW IN SPORT WHO HAVE PROVIDED MORE SUBLIME MOMENTS FOR THE PHOTOGRAPHERS TO WHOM THIS BOOK IS DEDICATED. MY FAVOURITE, PORTRAYED HERE, SHOWS HIM AFTER THE 1500 METRES WHICH COMPLETED HIS VICTORY IN THE 1982 EUROPEAN CHAMPIONSHIPS. AT HIS FEET, PROSTRATE ON THE TRACK, ARE THOSE HE HAD VANQUISHED. ONLY THOMPSON IS LEFT STANDING. IT ALWAYS SEEMED HIGHLY SYMBOLIC UNTIL THE MAN HIMSELF TOOK THE TROUBLE TO EXPLAIN IT. "I WAS STANDING BECAUSE THEY'D LEFT NO ROOM FOR ME TO LIE DOWN."

IT WAS A MOMENT EVEN HE COULD NOT HAVE REHEARSED. LIKE THE TIME I BEAT HIM AT SNOOKER.

NEIL WILSON THE INDEPENDENT

CONCENTRATION BY DALEY THOMPSON (LEFT) EN ROUTE TO HIS SECOND OLYMPIC GOLD IN LOS ANGELES, 1984.
VICTORY (RIGHT), IN THE EUROPEAN CHAMPIONSHIPS, 1982. PHOTOGRAPHS BY STEVE POWELL.

WORLD CUP CRICKET FINAL.
THE DELIRIUM OF INDIA'S SUPPORTERS FOLLOWING THEIR SHOCK VICTORY OVER THE MIGHTY WEST INDIES AT LORD'S IN **1983.** PHOTOGRAPH BY ADRIAN MURRELL.

THE SWEDISH WOMEN'S
RELAY TEAM, 1986 WORLD SWIM-
MING CHAMPIONSHIPS, MADRID.
PHOTOGRAPH BY TONY DUFFY.

KATARINA WITT, OF EAST
GERMANY: EUROPEAN, WORLD AND
OLYMPIC ICE-QUEEN.
PHOTOGRAPH BY YANN GUICHAOUA.

JOHN WATSON (ABOVE) PREPARES FOR THE 1977 MONACO
GRAND PRIX. PHOTOGRAPH BY TONY DUFFY. AYRTON SENNA, OF
BRAZIL (RIGHT), TAKES THE CURVE AT THE 1987 DETROIT GRAND
PRIX. PHOTOGRAPH BY BERNARD ASSET.

EMBRACE OF TRIUMPH. VALERIE BRISCO-HOOKS AND FLORENCE GRIFFITH (ABOVE), FINISH FIRST AND SECOND IN THE WOMEN'S 200 METRES AT THE 1984 LOS ANGELES OLYMPICS. PHOTOGRAPH BY STEVE POWELL. ALEXANDRE WORISCH OF AUSTRIA (RIGHT), SHEER BEAUTY AT THE 1981 EUROPEAN SWIMMING CHAMPIONSHIPS, YUGOSLAVIA. PHOTOGRAPH BY TONY DUFFY.

THE MOMENT OF PUSHING BACK THE BARRIER, TREADING FURTHER INTO NO MAN'S LAND, IS ONE SHARED IN THE SPORT OF ATHLETICS BY THE COMPETITOR AND SPECTATOR. ELATION FLOWS AND BONDS EVERYONE IN A MEMORY OF A WORLD RECORD TO BE TREASURED. BUT ON THE EVENING OF OCTOBER 18 1968, IN THE OLYMPIC ARENA OF MEXICO CITY, THERE WAS A NEW MIXTURE OF SENSATIONS AS BOB BEAMON ACHIEVED WHAT HAS SINCE SIMPLY BECOME KNOWN AS THE JUMP.

HIS PERFORMANCE STUNNED ALL, CAUSED DISBELIEF, DISTRACTION AMONG COMPETITORS WHO SUDDENLY FELT LIKE CHILDREN. BEAMON WAS LEFT IN WHAT DOCTORS LATER DESCRIBED A "CATAPLECTIC SEIZURE" AND HIS RIVALS HAD TO LIFT HIM TO HIS FEET TO HELP OVERCOME THE DIZZINESS AND NAUSEA, BROUGHT ON BY THE EMOTION OF IT ALL. SOMEHOW THE GREATEST PERFORMANCE IN ATHLETIC HISTORY HAD CREATED A KIND OF ANTI-ELATION. IN PART THERE WAS THE FEELING, WITH WHICH THE RECORD AND THE PERFORMER HAVE HAD TO LIVE, OF UNFAIRNESS. SET AGAINST THAT, HOWEVER, WAS THE SHEER ROMANTICISM BEHIND THE JUMP.

MEXICO CITY DISTORTED NORMAL ATHLETIC VALUES. MEN AND WOMEN FROM THE LOWLANDS WHO TRIED FOR MIDDLE AND LONG DISTANCE PRIZES AT AN ALTITUDE OF OVER 7,000 FEET, FOUND THE THINNESS OF THE ATMOSPHERE LIKE A TOURNIQUET AT THEIR CHEST. BUT IT WAS THAT THINNESS, 27 PER CENT ATMOSPHERIC PRESSURE AND 23 PER CENT LESS DENSITY, WHICH MEANT THAT, WITH HIS 100 METRES SPEED, BEAMON WAS ALMOST CERTAIN TO LEAP INTO HISTORY. INDEED, WITH JUST A CURSORY SCIENTIFIC KNOWLEDGE OF THE ADVANTAGES, HE FORECAST HE WOULD BREAK THE WORLD RECORD. WHY THEN, DID OTHERS FAIL TO DO SO? THE ANSWER IS THAT HE WAS THE FIRST MAN TO ACHIEVE A VALID JUMP (THE PREVIOUS THREE FOULED) AND HIS ENORMOUS ACHIEVEMENT SHATTERED ALL THOUGHTS OF CHALLENGE, BY MEN SUCH AS LYNN DAVIES, THE CHAMPION OF 1964, IGOR TER-OVANESIAN, OF THE SOVIET UNION, AND RALPH BOSTON, BEAMON'S COLLEAGUE. "YOU HAVE DESTROYED THE EVENT", BOSTON TOLD BEAMON WITHIN MOMENTS OF THE FEAT BEING MEASURED, FORGETTING THAT HE WAS A PART OF THAT DESTRUCTION.

IF BEAMON WAS THE VIRTUOSO, THEN BOSTON WAS, AT LEAST, THE IMPRESARIO. BEAMON WAS NATURALLY ATHLETIC BUT NOT MUCH OF A TECHNICIAN. HE HAD NEGLECTED SUCH ESSENTIALS AS CHECK MARKS ON THE RUNWAY AND IT SHOWED IN THE QUALIFYING ROUND, WHEN HIS FIRST JUMP WAS LUDICROUSLY OVER THE TAKE-OFF BOARD, BY ABOUT A FOOT, AND HE FOULED THE SECOND; HE HAD TO GET THE THIRD ONE IN OR HE WOULD HAVE BEEN ELIMINATED. HE WAS IN A TENSE STATE; BOSTON, HIS FRIEND, CALMED HIM DOWN AND TOLD HIM TO MARK A PLACE BEFORE THE TAKE-OFF BOARD AND AIM FOR IT. HE DID JUST THAT AND SO SLIPPED THROUGH THE NET TOWARDS ATHLETIC HISTORY.

IN THE FINAL THE FOLLOWING DAY, HE CONCENTRATED ON NOT FOULING HIS FIRST JUMP, FLEW DOWN THE RUNWAY, HIT THE TAKE-OFF BOARD PERFECTLY AND DID NOT SEEM TO BE JUMPING THROUGH, SO MUCH AS CONTINUING, HIS RUN — THE SPEED SEEMED UNCANNILY SIMILAR — AND HE BOUNCED BACK OUT OF THE PIT OFF HIS LANDING, WHICH RARELY HAPPENS. THE WORLD RECORD WAS 27 FEET FOUR-AND-THREE-QUARTER INCHES. "THAT'S 28 FEET", BOSTON SAID TO DAVIES; HE WAS WRONG, OF COURSE. IT TOOK MANY HANGING MOMENTS TO MEASURE THE BEAMON JUMP, BECAUSE WHEN THE JUDGE SLID THE OPTICAL MEASURING SIGHT ALONG THE STEEL POLE, IT FELL OFF THE END WITH SOME DISTANCE STILL TO BE COVERED BEFORE BEAMON'S LANDING MARK. A TAPE WAS PRODUCED AND THE TRUTH WAS DISCOVERED. BEAMON HAD JUMPED THE STAGGERING DISTANCE OF 29 FEET TWO-AND-HALF INCHES, OR, AS IT IS BETTER KNOWN, 8.90 METRES.

THERE WERE SUSPICIONS THAT THE WIND READING OF 2.0 METRES, EXACTLY ON THE LEGAL LIMIT, MIGHT HAVE BEEN A MISREADING, BUT ALL THOSE NOTIONS AND THE BEWILDERMENT OF THAT EVENING HAVE PASSED. BEAMON'S RECORD REMAINS AND, UNLESS SOMEONE GOES BACK TO MEXICO CITY FOR A COMPETITION, MAY DO SO UNTIL THE END OF THE CENTURY. **JOHN RODDA** THE GUARDIAN

BOB BEAMON CREATES HISTORY . . . CREATES ALLSPORT. PHOTOGRAPH BY TONY DUFFY.

STRETCHING A POINT. THE ILLUSION OF WARP-DRIVE IS CREATED BY ELECTRONIC EXTENSION OF THE BACKGROUND TO KENNY ROBERTS (ABOVE). PHOTOGRAPH BY DON MORLEY. THE SAME TECHNIQUE IS APPLIED TO EDDIE CHEEVER (BELOW). PHOTOGRAPH BY SIMON BRUTY.

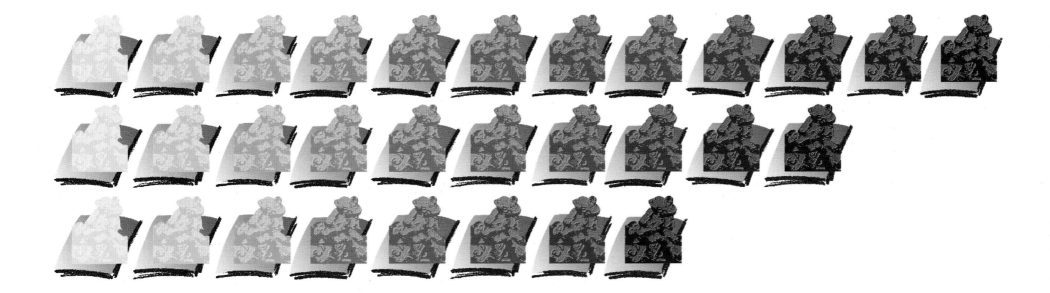

RUSHING. Chameleon-like, a pile of American football grid iron combatants change colour imperceptibly, but completely.

Photograph by Tony Duffy.

THE QUALITY OF REPRODUCTION in this book has been
made possible by Allsport's association with
Crosfield Electronics.
As leading suppliers to the Graphic Arts Industry, Crosfield has
used its expertise in digital image manipulation to
reproduce each and every picture in such a way as to capture
and sometimes enhance the atmosphere of the original
photograph.
The pictures on pages 152-155 use similar techniques,
pioneered by Crosfield, to electronically compose unique
sporting images with a new level of creativity and impact.

OUTSTANDING. THE INTIMACY OF THE RELATIONSHIP BETWEEN PLAYER AND SPECTATORS AT WIMBLEDON'S CENTRE COURT (LEFT) IS EMPHASISED BY THE USE OF ELECTRONIC MONTAGE TECHNIQUES. BORIS BECKER STANDS OUT FROM THE CROWD BUT IS ALSO PART OF IT. PHOTOGRAPH BY STEVE POWELL.

FLOATING. VALERIE BRISCO-HOOKS (ABOVE) RIDES THE MAGIC CARPET OF FULFILLED AMBITIONS. PHOTOGRAPH BY BOB MARTIN.

TONY DUFFY

TONY DUFFY.
BORN 1937, LONDON.
GAVE UP A CAREER AS A
CHARTERED ACCOUNTANT TO
CONCENTRATE ON HIS HOBBY,
SPORTS PHOTOGRAPHY, AFTER
TAKING THE PICTURE, WHILE A
TOURIST AT THE 1968 MEXICO
OLYMPICS, OF BOB BEAMON'S
WORLD RECORD BREAKING LONG-
JUMP. FOR MANY YEARS, ALLSPORT
WAS KNOWN AS "DUFFY'S AGENCY."
HIS INNOVATIVE WORK, INCLUDING
SUCH FEATURES AS "SPORT AND
THE BODY," SUNDAY TIMES, 1973,
INTRODUCED ALLSPORT TO A WIDER
AUDIENCE. THE USE OF NAKED
SPORTS STARS CAUSED UPROAR
AND BROUGHT NATIONWIDE
PUBLICITY. VOTED BRITISH SPORTS
PHOTOGRAPHER OF THE YEAR
(SPORTS COUNCIL/ROYAL
PHOTOGRAPHIC SOCIETY) IN 1975
AND HAS WON NUMEROUS
INTERNATIONAL AWARDS
INCLUDING INTERNATIONAL SPORTS
PICTURE OF THE YEAR IN 1975, 1977
AND 1981. MOVED TO LOS ANGELES
IN 1983 TO SET UP ALLSPORT
PHOTOGRAPHY USA.

ADRIAN MURRELL

ADRIAN MURRELL.
BORN 1955, TUNBRIDGE WELLS.
BEGAN WORK AS A FREELANCE
SPORTS PHOTOGRAPHER AND,
AFTER COVERING ENGLAND'S TOUR
TO INDIA IN 1977, DECIDED TO
SPECIALISE IN CRICKET. HAS BEEN
"SPECIAL PHOTOGRAPHER" FOR THE
CRICKETER MAGAZINE SINCE THEN,
AND, APART FROM THE RECENT
TOUR TO NEW ZEALAND (1988),
HAS COVERED EVERY ENGLAND
OVERSEAS TOUR. JOINED ALLSPORT
IN 1979. ILFORD SPORTS
PHOTOGRAPHER OF THE YEAR IN
1981 AND IN 1985 WON THE
BENSON AND HEDGES CRICKET
PHOTOGRAPHER OF THE YEAR.
HIGHLY COMMENDED FOR HIS
PORTFOLIO IN THE SPORTS
PHOTOGRAPHER OF THE YEAR
(SPORTS COUNCIL/ROYAL
PHOTOGRAPHIC SOCIETY) IN 1977
AND 1985. BECAME MANAGING
DIRECTOR OF ALLSPORT UK IN
DECEMBER 1986.

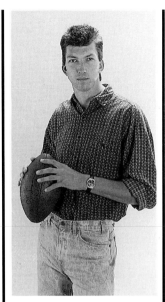

GERARD VANDYSTADT

GERARD VANDYSTADT.
BORN 1948, PARIS.
AT 15, HE SAW HIS FIRST PUBLISHED
PHOTOGRAPH APPEAR ON THE
FRONT PAGE OF A NATIONAL
NEWSPAPER IN FRANCE.
FOLLOWING THIS PRECOCIOUS
SUCCESS HE WORKED WITH A
NUMBER OF NEWSPAPERS AND
MAGAZINES AS A PHOTO-
JOURNALIST AND LATER, AFTER
BECOMING A FULL-TIME
PHOTOGRAPHER, DISTRIBUTED HIS
SPORTS PICTURES VIA PRESS
AGENCIES, TO NATIONAL AND
INTERNATIONAL MAGAZINES. IN
1977 HE FOUNDED HIS OWN
SPORTS PICTURE AGENCY, AGENCE
VANDYSTADT, WHICH HAS SINCE
BECOME THE MOST IMPORTANT
AGENCY IN FRANCE. SINCE 1983 HE
HAS ALSO BEEN THE DIRECTOR OF
ALLSPORT FRANCE.
HE SPECIALISES IN ATHLETICS AND
FREESTYLE ICE-SKATING.

MIKE POWELL

MIKE POWELL.
BORN 1965, ALDERSHOT.
JOINED ALLSPORT IN 1982 AS
DARKROOM AND LIBRARY JUNIOR,
SHOOTING MINOR SPORTS AT
WEEKENDS. BY 1985 HAD
GRADUATED TO JUNIOR
PHOTOGRAPHER WITH SUCH JOBS
AS THE EUROPEAN SWIMMING
CHAMPIONSHIPS, RAC RALLY, LE
MANS, AUSTRALIAN RUGBY TOUR
OF UK AND ON THE FORMULA ONE
GRAND PRIX CIRCUIT. MOVED TO
LOS ANGELES IN 1985 TO WORK
WITH TONY DUFFY AS A SENIOR
PHOTOGRAPHER, COVERING SPORTS
SUCH AS BASEBALL, BASKETBALL,
AMERICAN FOOTBALL AND BOXING
INCLUDING THE MIKE TYSON
VERSUS TREVOR BERBICK WORLD
HEAVYWEIGHT TITLE FIGHT.

RUSSELL CHEYNE

RUSSELL CHEYNE.
BORN 1963, GLASGOW.
AFTER TRAINING AT RICHMOND
COLLEGE, SHEFFIELD WORKED AS A
FREELANCE FOR RANGERS NEWS IN
GLASGOW. SPENT ONE YEAR AT
MERCURY PRESS AGENCY,
LIVERPOOL, AND JOINED ALLSPORT
IN 1986. SPECIALISES IN RUGBY
AND SOCCER. HE WAS HIGHLY
COMMENDED IN THE 1987 SPORT
FOR ALL AWARDS, AND HIS WORK
HAS BEEN PUBLISHED IN
THE SUNDAY TIMES,
SUNDAY TELEGRAPH AND
OBSERVER MAGAZINES.

THE MAJORITY OF PHOTOGRAPHS IN THIS BOOK WERE TAKEN WITH KODAK PROFESSIONAL PRODUCTS.

PHOTOGRAPHS BY JOHN GICHIGI

OLI TENNENT

OLI TENNENT.
BORN 1963, LONDON.
STUDIED PHOTOGRAPHY AT BOURNEMOUTH ART COLLEGE AND FREELANCED FOR TWO YEARS BEFORE JOINING ALLSPORT IN 1987. INITIALLY SPECIALISED IN MOTOR-CYCLE RACING, BUT NOW REGARDED AS A LEADER IN THE FIELD OF POWERBOAT RACING PHOTOGRAPHY. HAS COVERED SAILING/WATER SPORTS EVENTS IN FLORIDA, DUBAI, HAWAII AND NEW ZEALAND. HIS WORK HAS BEEN PUBLISHED IN MAGAZINES FROM BRAZIL TO HONG KONG.

SIMON BRUTY

SIMON BRUTY.
BORN 1965, PORTSMOUTH.
JOINED ALLSPORT 1984. HAS TRAVELLED EXTENSIVELY DURING THE PAST TWO YEARS, COVERING SUCH DIVERSE EVENTS AS THE BRAZILIAN GRAND PRIX IN RIO DE JANEIRO, RYDER CUP GOLF, GRID IRON FOOTBALL IN THE UNITED STATES, AND A SOLAR-POWERED CAR RACE IN AUSTRALIA AS WELL AS INTERNATIONAL AND DOMESTIC FOOTBALL ALL OVER EUROPE. HIGHLY COMMENDED IN THE 1987 SPORTS PHOTOGRAPHER OF THE YEAR COMPETITION (SPORTS COUNCIL/ROYAL PHOTOGRAPHIC SOCIETY). IN 1988, COVERED ENGLAND'S CRICKET TOUR TO NEW ZEALAND FOR THE OBSERVER.

BOB MARTIN

BOB MARTIN.
BORN 1959, LONDON.
STARTED CAREER WITH A GROUP OF WEDDING PHOTOGRAPHERS BASED IN TEDDINGTON AS A PRINT DRIER. THEN, WHILE WORKING IN THE PHOTOGRAPHIC UNIT OF THE CIVIL ENGINEERING DEPARTMENT AT IMPERIAL COLLEGE, LONDON, HE ALSO STUDIED PHOTOGRAPHY AT RICHMOND COLLEGE OF TECHNOLOGY. JOINED ALLSPORT IN 1978 AS A GENERAL SPORTS PHOTOGRAPHER, LATER CONCENTRATING ON ATHLETICS AND TENNIS. NOW ALSO SPECIALISES IN ELINCHROM LIGHTING TECHNIQUES AT MAJOR ATHLETICS MEETINGS.

DAVID CANNON

DAVID CANNON.
BORN 1955, LONDON.
PLAYED THE AMATEUR GOLF CIRCUIT FOR FIVE YEARS AFTER LEAVING SCHOOL IN OXFORD IN 1973. HIS FIRST JOB WAS AS A SALESMAN BUT AFTER A BOUT OF GLANDULAR FEVER, THREE MONTHS' PAID LEAVE, A FIRST SLR CAMERA AND AN INTRODUCTION TO THE LEICESTER NEWS AGENCY PHOTOGRAPHIC STUDIO, HE WAS ON HIS WAY. SPECIALISING IN FOOTBALL WHILE WORKING FOR A NORTHERN PICTURE AGENCY, HE WAS INVITED TO JOIN ALLSPORT IN 1983, SINCE WHEN HE HAS MAINTAINED AN INTEREST IN SOCCER BUT ALSO RETURNED TO HIS ROOTS AS ALLSPORT'S GOLF PHOTOGRAPHER.

STEVE POWELL AND LUCIE

STEVE POWELL.
BORN 1952, LONDON.
JOINED KEYSTONE PRESS AGENCY FROM SCHOOL. FIRST INTERESTED IN PHOTO-NEWS JOURNALISM AND, WHILE AT KEYSTONE, WAS SENT TO COVER EVENTS IN NORTHERN IRELAND. MET AND STARTED WORKING WITH TONY DUFFY IN 1970 AND JOINED HIM FULL-TIME IN 1971.
DEVELOPED HIS CAREER WORKING FOR SEVERAL INTERNATIONAL SPORTS MAGAZINES, NOTABLY SPORTS ILLUSTRATED, SPECIALISING IN ATHLETICS AND WINTER SPORTS. ALSO RESPONSIBLE FOR THE DEVELOPMENT OF THE AGENCY AND ITS INTERNATIONAL ROLE, THE COMPUTERISATION AND RE-LOCATION OF THE COMPANY TO PRESENT HEADQUARTERS IN LONDON SW19. HIGHLY COMMENDED IN NUMEROUS NATIONAL AND INTERNATIONAL SPORTS PHOTOGRAPHY AWARDS. WINNER OF THE AMERICAN BEST SPORTS STORY AWARD IN 1982 AND COLOUR SPORTS PHOTOGRAPHER OF THE YEAR IN 1985. NOW GROUP MANAGING DIRECTOR.

OTHER CONTRIBUTING PHOTOGRAPHERS:

BERNARD ASSET
JEAN-MARC BAREY
GUIDO BENETTON
CHRISTIAN LE BOZEC
CHRIS COLE
YANN GUICHAOUA
YANN ARTHUS BERTRAND
JOHN GICHIGI
TONY INZERILLO
TREVOR JONES
MIKE KING
JEAN-MARC LOUBAT
DON MORLEY
CHRISTIAN PETIT
PASCAL RONDEAU
DAN SMITH

THE PHOTOGRAPHS PUBLISHED IN THIS BOOK HAVE BEEN SELECTED FROM
MORE THAN 4 MILLION TRANSPARENCIES HELD BY THE ALLSPORT AGENCIES
IN BRITAIN, AMERICA AND FRANCE.
THANKS ARE EXPRESSED TO EVERYONE WHO, THROUGH THE 20 YEARS OF
ALLSPORT'S EXISTENCE, HAVE CONTRIBUTED TO THE AGENCY'S SUCCESS.

DETAILS OF ALLSPORT'S THREE MAIN AGENCIES ARE:

ALLSPORT PHOTOGRAPHIC PLC, LONDON
3, GREENLEA PARK, PRINCE GEORGE'S ROAD,
LONDON SW19 2JD
ENGLAND
TELEPHONE: (01) 685 1010 TELEX: 8955022 ASPORT G
FAX: (01) 648 5240
GROUP MANAGING DIRECTOR: STEVE POWELL

ALLSPORT PHOTOGRAPHY USA INC, LOS ANGELES
SUITE 200
320 WILSHIRE BOULEVARD, SANTA MONICA, LOS ANGELES, CA 90401, USA
TELEPHONE: (213) 395 2955 TELEX: 697937
FAX: (213) 394 6099
PRESIDENT: TONY DUFFY

ALLSPORT FRANCE/AGENCE VANDYSTADT, PARIS
61-63 RUE DES ENTREPRENEURS, 75015 PARIS, FRANCE
TELEPHONE: (1) 45 79 88 54 TELEX: 206928 F VANDY
FAX: (1) 45 75 32 71
DIRECTOR: GERARD VANDYSTADT

PLUS AN INTERNATIONAL NETWORK OF 30 AGENTS THROUGHOUT THE FIVE CONTINENTS.